A PARTING OF THE WAYS

"He won't get far in there," Spock commented as he and Kirk headed for the dense thicket. His estimate was reasonable as far as it went, but it didn't go far enough to include a Pandronian.

Commander bn Bem came up against a veritable dead end, a place where the small trees grew so close together that no one of his size could possibly squeeze through. So, the commander did what any good Pandronian would do—he split into three parts, each of which was small enough to ooze through any of several openings in the wood.

Once successfully past the barrier the tripartite alien promptly reassembled himself and continued blithely on his composite way.

STAR TREK
LOG NINE

Alan Dean Foster

Based on the Popular Animated Series Created
by Gene Roddenberry

BALLANTINE BOOKS • NEW YORK

For Charlie Lippincott,
with admiration and friendship

Library of Congress Catalog Card Number: 74-8477

ISBN 0-345-25557-7-150

Manufactured in the United States of America

First Edition: February 1977

STAR TREK LOG NINE

Log of the Starship *Enterprise*

Stardates 5537.3–5537.9 Inclusive

James T. Kirk, Capt., USSC, FC, ret.

Commanding

transcribed by
Alan Dean Foster

At the Galactic Historical Archives
on Ursa Major Lacus
stardated 6111.3

For the Curator: JLR

BEM

(Adapted from a script by David Gerrold)

"Captain's log, stardate 5537.3."

Kirk directed his voice toward the log recorder as he settled himself more comfortably in the command chair. "The *Enterprise,* having concluded the Lactran affair and having returned officers Markel, Bryce, and Randolph to Starbase Sixteen Survey Headquarters, is proceeding according to directives on standard survey run." As Kirk shut off the recorder, he decided this mission wasn't *quite* standard.

With all ship's operations functioning smoothly, he was able to lean back and relax slightly. The small portable reader screen set into the left-hand chair arm was playing back an ancient history of Starfleet. Presently the screen displayed the half-legendary story of how one Matthew Jeffries first conceived of the Constitution Class vessels, of which the *Enterprise* was but one of many now.

Fascinating as the tale was, wreathed in myth and the uncertain garb of Terran history, Kirk soon found his mind wandering. He had originally intended to pause at Base 16 and add his own personal observations and comments to the report of the rescued survey team. Instead, he had to settle for submitting the appropriate taped report and excerpts from the ship's log. As usual, the completion of one mission meant that half a dozen more awaited the *Enterprise* in the backlog of Starfleet's central computer network. There were never enough ships, never adequate personnel available

1

to handle the continually growing task of taking some of the mystery from newly discovered worlds.

The Federation's tireless drone probes, immune to fatigue, had recently located several previously unknown and closely packed systems of planets and satellites. These potential colony worlds required the kind of in-depth, and thorough, preliminary study only a major-class starship could provide. So the *Enterprise* was immediately dispatched to carry out routine observations.

At least, the journey would be as routine as one could expect with the opening up of several new worlds—each one filled with a googolplex of new problems and dangers and promises. There would be one other small break in routine—one minor alteration in assigned personnel. An extra, official observer had been added to the roster for the duration of the mission. What made him important was not that he was nonhuman, non-Vulcan, and even nonhumanoid, but that he was a representative of a recently contacted intelligent race.

The orders Kirk had received went on to explain that the Federation was going through a very delicate stage in its relations with the government of Commander Ari bn Bem, of the system of Pandro. The Pandronians had requested that a representative of theirs be permitted to observe a Federation crew carrying out precisely the type of mission the *Enterprise* had just been assigned.

Such simple requests could not be refused. According to his orders, both the Klingons and the Romulans had expressed an interest in deepening their ties with the Pandronians. Every opportunity should be taken to convince the Pandronians that their interests would best be served by a close alliance with the Federation, particularly since several Federation worlds existed in a strategic position relative to Pandro. What all that meant was that Pandro held a position of vital concern to several Federation worlds—but the official phrasing of spatial relationships was more, ah, realistic.

Federation DIPS—members of the Diplomatic Psychology Corps—were convinced that the Federation was gaining the upper hand in the battle for Pandronian influence—a battle that had to be augmented by the cooperation and aid of everyone in Starfleet. Captain Kirk was therefore directed to extend to Commander bn Bem all courtesies normally extended to an attached observer, with special regard for the precarious diplomatic situation, keeping in mind the need to . . .

Et cetera, et cetera.

Well, Kirk had it in mind, all right! The matter had been foremost in his mind since that always underfoot, irritating, and occasionally downright rude Pandronian had come aboard. Unless something happened to change their visitor's attitude, Kirk feared that Federation-Pandronian relations could be severely damaged. He was also afraid that Commander bn Bem might be severely damaged. The list of angry complaints from insulted or challenged or otherwise provoked crew members was approaching critical mass.

He managed to shove the problem from his thoughts as he added a short entry to the log. The view now on the main screen—a handsome world of swirling white clouds and blue ocean—did much to blank out all thoughts of their obstreperous visitor.

"Captain's log, stardate 5537.3. We are taking up orbit around Delta Theta Three, a newly charted Class M planet—the last world on our current mission. The original drone scout reported the possible presence of aboriginal life forms on Delta Theta Three, life forms of undetermined intelligence and accomplishment.

"Upon entering orbit the *Enterprise* will proceed to carry out standard survey procedures and investigation, placing particular emphasis on a detailed study of the local sapient life form."

Kirk clicked off the machine as he rose, heading for the turbolift. The presence of even a marginally intelligent life form would be a most welcome conclusion to this expedition, which had been remarkable only for the mediocrity and unattractiveness of the worlds they had examined thus far.

And then there was the remarkable unattractiveness of the singularly trying Commander bn Bem. The Pandronian was one guest Kirk would be glad to be rid of. As he rode the lift toward the Transporter Room, he broke out in a satisfied smile at the thought of the moment when Commander bn Bem would be officially returned to the Pandronian mission at Starbase 13.

He came upon the rest of the initial landing party in the corridor leading to the Transporter Room—Sulu, and Spock, with Scott accompanying them.

"Anything new on your potential hosts, Captain?" Scott called to him.

"Sensors have located several possible groupings of aborigines, Scotty," Kirk informed them. "The xenologists are sure of one thing—Delta Theta Three isn't another world of superminds like Lactra. The natives here are definitely primitive. Bear in mind, gentlemen, that like all primitive peoples they may tend to spear first and think later. I want everyone to keep in mind that no unnecessary risks are to be taken, no matter how important the information in question." He indicated the compact, cylindrical instruments each man held.

"These monitoring devices have to be hand-planted close to a center of local activity, if we're going to get any long-term data on these people. That accomplished, we'll beam up. Study of flora and fauna, geological features, and the like can be best accomplished by specialized teams afterwards.

"Lieutenant Uhura will be tracking us throughout, and Mr. Kyle will be standing by." Chief Engineer Scott nodded reassuringly. "If there is trouble of any kind, beam up immediately. Don't try to be a hero, and don't place intelligence gathering above your own life." This last comment was directed, as usual, at Spock, who, as usual, took no notice.

As the door sensed their approach, it slid aside, admitting them to the Transporter Room. Entering, they started toward the transporter alcove—and froze. Chief Kyle was present, but not in his accustomed position behind the console. Instead, he stood to one side, uncertainly eyeing the creature who occupied his station. At the entrance of the captain and his companions, Kyle turned and threw Kirk a helpless look.

Kirk nodded once as he turned his attention to the console. The biped who stood behind it, fiddling with every control in reach, was more or less of human size. Resemblance to anything manlike faded rapidly after that. The creature was bulky, blue, and hirsute—all three characteristics amply apparent despite the concealing full-length uniform it wore. The interloper had also noted the entrance of the four officers and turned to bestow the toothy equivalent of a Pandronian grin on an unamused Kirk.

"Ah, Kirk Captain," he rumbled in a voice like a contrabassoon full of marbles, "welcome and greeting. Settings are almost complete."

For the moment Kirk elected to ignore the Pandronian's unauthorized manipulation of the transporter controls. And there was no reason to reprimand Kyle, who had only been following the orders regarding bn Bem. As honorary Federation commander, the visiting Pandronian had free run of the cruiser. The mounting stack of complaints back in Kirk's office attested to the extent to which bn Bem had exercised his privileges.

Ordered to stand aside by a "superior" officer, Kyle had done so. The transporter engineer would have his chance to report on this incident later. At the moment, it was the Pandronian's presence which concerned Kirk most.

"Commander bn Bem, exactly what are you doing here? I thought you would be down in Sciences, studying procedure as information on the world below is gathered."

bn Bem replied readily in the highly contemptuous manner which perfectly complemented his personality. It was almost, Kirk reflected, as if the Pandronian were granting them a gigantic favor by deigning to grace the *Enterprise* with his presence. "This One," bn Bem sneered, "has decided to accompany contact team for observation of Delta Theta surface."

Kirk ignored the tone of the envoy's voice. He had

learned these past days to tune it out. Nevertheless, he couldn't keep all trace of irritation from his reply. "Commander bn Bem," he reminded the other with as much control as he could muster, "you were assigned to this ship in an 'attached observer' status. Yet you've spent the past several planetary circumnavigations holed up in your quarters—when you weren't intruding for 'observation' into the private quarters of my crew. You haven't made anything like a detailed study of our survey methods—until now, it seems, when we are about to deal with a world that may very well sport a hostile primitive culture."

bn Bem's answer took the form of a controlled, basso chirp, made softly, but just loud enough for Kirk and the others to hear. "Patience . . . every planet is dangerous to the ignorant." Now speaking in a normal conversational tone, he resumed. "This One has decided that the nexus is now. Must now observe workings of starship and crew. This One is not impressed by outside recommendations for study time. A teacher is not instructed by students."

"You've had ample opportunity to 'observe workings' both on board and on-surface during our last several planetfalls—at all times in comparative safety. This beam-down is not for the casual observer, especially one as diplomatically sensitive as you know you are. It could be hazardous and—"

"I am prepared," bn Bem countered simply.

Kirk started to say something, turned, then muttered to his first officer. "Mr. Spock, I don't like this at all. Diplomatic relations could be endangered if anything happens to this—this—to Commander bn Bem while he's our guest."

"It is not merely political considerations that dictate our actions, Captain," Spock reminded him. "There is the fact that the Pandronians are also very advanced in certain exotic areas of medicine and biology. There is much we can learn from them—much that Starfleet would rather we learned than the Klingons, say. And remember—orders expressly stated that Commander bn Bem be given anything he requested."

"Within reason," Kirk added. "But I don't think this request to join the landing party is reasonable."

"Starfleet may feel otherwise."

Kirk started to offer further objection, but found Spock's reminder inarguable. He let out a frustrated, heartfelt sigh and turned back to their guest. He'd make one last try.

"Commander bn Bem, this is not going to be a pleasure excursion. I really cannot, in clear conscience, permit you to beam down to this planet with us. You understand my position, I'm sure."

"Understanding it is," bn Bem replied, "but dirty conscience if required. This one is adamant and bystanding to accompany on landing."

Kirk growled back, wondering at the Pandronian's perverse preferences. "This is an odd time to be adamant."

There wasn't much Kirk could do about it, except say no—and that could undo all the courtesy they had so painfully extended to bn Bem thus far. "All right," he finally grumbled, "let's go. There's a world waiting for us." He stomped toward the transporter alcove.

"Scotty, if you'll set—"

bn Bem interrupted him even as the chief engineer was moving to the console. bn Bem was an accomplished interrupter. "Waste not the time. This One has already controls set, Mr. Scotty."

"Mr. Scotty" eyed the Pandronian distrustfully and proceeded to make an elaborate, overthorough inspection of the settings in question. Hard squints and florid gestures notwithstanding, he was finally compelled to look toward the alcove and nod slowly.

"Everythin' appears to be okay, Captain," he announced. "The coordinates are locked in on the preselected touchdown site, and everythin' else looks proper."

bn Bem let out a snort of satisfaction, which no one could fail to hear—least of all Scott—before taking his place in the alcove next to Kirk, Spock, and Sulu. "Time waste," he muttered disgustedly. His human companions resolutely ignored him.

They were joined a moment later by Scott as Kyle assumed the position behind the transporter console. Kirk checked to make certain everyone still held the important automatic monitoring devices, then nodded toward the console.

"Energize, Chief."

The room faded around them. . . .

Delta Theta Three was a name devoid of planetary personality, but the little group was soon to discover the world so designated was well equipped with same.

All at once five roughly cylindrical forms of glowing particles appeared near the shore of a lake and commenced to coalesce.

The lake itself was covered with brown scum and riotous blue growths, shading in color almost to black in places. Equally bloated vegetation thrived in the swampy region draining into the lake. A meandering stream entered the lake to the right of the rapidly solidifying figures, the water drifting with infinite slowness. Black and brown cypresslike trees, long creepers, and twisting vines occupied much of the open space between the larger boles. But despite the luxuriant growth, there was an absence of grass and ground cover, giving the jungle an underlying appearance of desolation.

The few open, meadowed spaces were muddy and unwholesome-looking. In contrast to the somewhat ominous landscape, the cries of innumerable tiny climbers and other hidden creatures sounded merrily from within the thickly overgrown areas.

The five cylinder-shapes became more distinct, added detail and resolution, and turned into the five explorers transported from the *Enterprise*. Something caused a split-second delay in the final transformation of each figure. Scott resolved first, stumbling slightly as he did so on the soft, sloping shoreline. Sulu appeared next to him, stumbling awkwardly enough to fall momentarily to his knees.

bn Bem was next. The Pandronian actually materialized a full meter above the shore, which did not affect him as the slight difference had affected Scott and Sulu. His legs instinctively extended the additional meter to allow him a gentle setdown. Once established on the ground, those elastic limbs retracted to their normal length. No one saw the startling adaptation take place.

Kirk and Spock completed the arrival of the landing party. They rematerialized at a similar distance above the water. Having neither extendable legs, nor wings, the two looked both confused and stunned as they dropped, making a pair of undignified splashes. Fortunately the water was only chest deep.

As the only one of the arrivals with a sound footing on land, bn Bem rushed into the water to aid the struggling Kirk and Spock in regaining their footing. Kirk had already suspected their guest of having a many-layered personality, but a multilayered torso was something no one could have anticipated.

The Pandronians were a *very* new race to Federation biologists. Consequently, neither the captain, nor the rapidly righting Spock—much less Sulu or Scott—took note that under the murky surface Commander bn Bem's lower half detached itself from his upper torso with all the ease and naturalness of a shuttle leaving the *Enterprise*'s hanger.

While the creature's upper half made arm motions to aid the floundering Kirk, the lower half swam busily around behind the captain and proceeded to remove his phaser and communicator. These devices were immediately and efficiently replaced with well-made copies. Then the substitution was carried out on Spock.

Above, bn Bem—half of him, anyway—entended an arm as Kirk regained his balance. "Assistance is offered," he said, with barely concealed distaste.

Kirk and his first officer exchanged glances, then Kirk looked back at their guest. "Thanks just the same, Commander. We'll manage."

bn Bem imitated a human shrug, one of his newly acquired gestures. "As you choose." As he turned to leave the water, his lower half reattached itself to the upper. It was an intact and familiar Pandronian who emerged from the lake.

Kirk and Spock struggled out of the plant-choked stagnant water, both completely unaware that anything untoward had taken place. If they had felt a slight twinge or two, they might have looked more closely at the slight bulges in the Pandronian's sample pouch, dangling loosely from one hip. The pouch looked full, which was odd if one considered they hadn't been here long enough to do much sampling.

Kirk choked back the thousand or so suggestions that sprang immediately to the tip of his tongue and contented himself with saying, "In the future, Commander bn Bem, you will leave the operation of the transporter to Mr. Scott, Mr. Kyle, or one of the regular members of the transporter crew."

"Is response to offer of aid," bn Bem murmured. "Typical." He seemed ready to add a few additional choice observations, but was interrupted himself for a change.

"Captain!"

Kirk looked at the anxious expression on his chief engineer's face. "What's the matter, Scotty?" He shook water from his arms and began stripping the clinging water plants from his tunic, hoping that soggy mess didn't contain anything likely to bite, cut, or otherwise make a nuisance of itself at some future date.

"Maybe nothing, Captain," Scott replied, "but Lieutenant Uhura reports some very unusual activity in our general vicinity."

Wonderful! They had barely touched down, and already they'd gotten drenched to the skin and were now confronted with something else unexpected. He took a couple of steps and hefted the open communicator.

"What kind of activity, Lieutenant?"

Uhura spoke from her position as commander-in-charge, leaning forward toward the con pickup. "Lieutenant Arex has been tracking what appears to be a mobile nonnetwork sensory stasis. It's still very small," she added after looking for confirmation to Arex seated at Navigation, "and it's several thousand kilometers west of your present position."

Kirk frowned. "Say again, Lieutenant?"

Uhura's voice was only slightly distorted, thanks to the ever efficient communicator. "It resembles a ship's sensor field, but there's nothing detectable like a scanning grid or other central point of reference."

Kirk digested this information, his concern mitigated by the distance involved. "You said it was mobile, Lieutenant. How mobile?"

"Lieutenant Arex speaking, sir," came the Edoan navigator's crisp tones. "Brownian movement only—no discernible direction and no hint of a guiding force."

"Most odd," Spock commented from nearby. "The implication is that there is something else on this world beyond aborigines. One would have to suspect something intelligent, yet nothing of the kind was reported in the initial survey." He shook his head. "It hardly seems likely the probes would have missed something we have detected so soon after arrival."

Kirk decided to ignore the implication, for the present. As long as whatever it was presented no immediate threat, they would concentrate on the task at hand. But he could no more stifle his curiosity than could Spock.

"It might be a very low-lying atmospheric anomaly, Mr. Spock. We've encountered other climatic phenomena before which have superficially resembled the activities of something sentient. And keep in mind that a drone probe isn't the most exacting observer. Detailed examination of a world is our business."

"None of which I had forgotten, Captain, and all of which I agree with."

Kirk turned back to the communicator. "Keep monitoring, Lieutenant Uhura. As a precaution only, put the ship on yellow alert. We'll continue the survey and monitor-emplacement mission for now, but notify us immediately if there is any change in the situation. An increase in the intensity of the field, a change of speed or direction, and especially anything that might indicate the field is under the control of intelligence—anything which hints that this might be other than a natural phenomenon. Kirk out."

He closed the communicator, breaking transmission,

and handed it back to Scott, then indicated a path through the swampy meadows. "According to the computer plotting, the nearest life-form concentration— presumably the nearest native village—is this way. Let's get on with it."

Footing near the lake ranged "from the oleaginous to the obfuscatory," as Spock pointed out. That remark prompted Scott to redefine it in less precise but more colorful terms.*

The ground they encountered was messy, but not dangerous. There were no quicksands or sandpits. After some hard slogging, they found themselves moving through the forest and meadows with confidence, if not comfort.

"The rain-forest ecology is particularly interesting here," Spock commented absorbedly. "Life on this planet appears to be geologically younger than one would expect, given the age of this star and—"

A familiar voice interrupted, almost on cue. "Now urgent." bn Bem was studying his own tricorder. "Announce: This One is picking up readings which indicate a large group of intelligent-maybes life forms directly ahead."

Kirk held up a hand and called for a halt. "All right. We must take care not to be seen. Part of the prime directive— Hey!"

Commander bn Bem, ignoring all instructions and precautions, took off at high speed toward the hypothesized aborigines.

"Commander bn Bem, come back!" Kirk shouted. He started off after the retreating figure. "Scotty, Sulu—stay here."

"But, Captain—" Scott began.

Kirk cut him off curtly. "Orders, Scotty. Stand by. Come on, Spock." They both broke into a run in pursuit of the galloping Pandronian.

Their bulky guest appeared to be slowing as they crossed a swampy meadow. He vanished into a clump

---

*Transcriber's note: Ethnic highland terminology omitted here by curator's directive.

of tightly packed black trunks laced with interweaving vines.

"He won't get far in there," Spock commented with satisfaction.

Kirk's reply was tense. "I hope not—for his own sake, as well as ours."

They headed for the dense thicket. Spock's estimate was reasonable as far as it went, but it did not go far enough to include a Pandronian.

bn Bem came up against a veritable dead end, a place where the small trees grew so close together that no one his size could possibly squeeze through. So the commander split into three parts, each of which was small enough to ooze through any of several openings in the wall of wood. Once successfully past the barrier the tripartite alien promptly reassembled himself and continued blithely on his composite way.

Unfortunately, neither Kirk nor Spock was capable of such bodily diffusion, nor was either aware that their recalcitrant guest was. They came to the same dead end, only in their case the description was fitting and final.

"He's gone," Kirk exclaimed, spinning to search every crevice, each potential hiding place.

But Spock continued to stare in disbelief straight ahead. "He could not have reversed his direction and slipped past us. To escape he had to go through here."

"That's impossible, Spock," Kirk said confidently, turning. "There's no way—" He stopped, moved to a gap in the trees the size of his chest, and stared through. He got only a brief glimpse of a blue bipedal figure disappearing into the distance. But unless this world was inhabited by blue, two-legged aborigines, Kirk had a pretty good idea who it was.

"There he is, all right." He frowned. "I don't know how he got through, but get through he did." Kirk took hold of the smallest trunk bordering the gap, got a good grip with both hands, braced himself, and gave a mighty heave. The tree moved about as much as one of the *Enterprise*'s warp-drive engines would under similar circumstances.

"Come on, Spock, we'll have to go around."

They began to circle the dense grove of saplings and vines, well aware that bn Bem could be far ahead by the time they found a way. Something else was puzzling Kirk.

"That Pandronian's actions just don't make sense. Never mind for the moment how he got through that tight space. Right now I'd like to know *why* he did it. No sense, none at all."

"His actions might make sense to another Pandronian, Captain," the always pragmatic Spock suggested.

"I suppose so," Kirk confessed. "I've got to admit that one thing I've never found it easy to understand are the motivations of another species."

"Indeed?" exclaimed his first officer, with an inflection that indicated there was something more to his remark.

They detoured until they reached a section of the closely bunched trees which was penetrable. The forest closed in around them, shutting out the meadow and nearly doing likewise to the sun. As it turned out, the intertwined trunks were a disguised blessing, for the surface here was too soft and deep to permit rapid walking. They made much better time through the branches.

"I believe that is the direction, Captain," Spock said finally, when the trees showed signs of thinning. "Or possibly it was more to the left. Or perhaps—"

"We've lost him," Kirk finished succinctly. He was studying the small open area ahead, equally uncertain which way to go, when he heard a low murmur off to their left.

"That way—something over there."

Some frenetic crawling and running brought them to a wide clearing. They were about to move out into the open by jumping a fallen log when each man's hand went to his companion's shoulder and the two dropped down behind it.

They had seen the movement simultaneously.

"It would appear to be a native food-gathering

party," Spock ventured, peering at the still-distant, slow-moving forms.

"Yes," agreed Kirk, "and part of the food they've gathered is Commander bn Bem."

At this distance it was difficult to obtain an accurate picture of the aborigines, but they appeared to stand just under an impressive three meters in height. Their skin was bright red; the overall impression was of reptilian, dull-witted, and probably belligerent creatures.

Commander bn Bem stood in their midst, looking decidedly unhappy. For the moment his usual haughtiness and air of self-satisfaction was completely absent.

Equally anxious minds studied the situation from more comfortable and more remote surroundings. Strange information was coming through on the *Enterprise*'s instruments. "Lieutenant Uhura," Arex finally declared, "I'm picking up mounting activity on the surface. Initial indications point to an expansion of the still unidentified sensory anomaly."

Uhura nodded, glanced backwards. "Lieutenant M'ress, contact the landing party."

"Aye, aye, Lieutenant."

Scott's gaze shifted from the placid surface of the vegatation-choked lake to his communicator as it buzzed urgently.

"Scott here."

"Mr. Scott, where's the captain?"

"He's separated from us. Commander bn Bem ran off into the forest and—"

"Ran off into the forest?" came Uhura's startled echo.

"Yes. I know it's undiplomatic of me, but I say good riddance. However, the captain's not in a position to do so. He's responsible for that hairy— Anyway, he and Mr. Spock took off after our Pandronian charge. They're out in the brush somewhere. Sulu and I were ordered to remain here." He looked into the trees, staring in the direction the two senior officers had taken too many minutes ago.

"That was a while ago, and it doesn't look very friendly down here." He chewed his lower lip. "Have you tried contacting them directly since they disappeared?"

"Yes, we have. Neither the captain nor Mr. Spock acknowledges his communicator. Nor," Uhura added, "do they show up on the scanning grid. We can detect only one energy source, and it hasn't moved. That would be you and Sulu.

"It's their absence on the grid that really worries me, Commander Scott. The silence almost screams that their communicator responders have been disconnected. Also, we're picking up increased sensory activity."

"The large anomaly?"

"Yes. Nothing threatening. At least, it's as unthreatening as something that big and inexplicable can be." Her voice turned firm. "You're certain Mr. Spock went with the captain?"

"Aye, Lieutenant."

Her voice faded slightly as she apparently addressed someone on the bridge. Scott heard the order faintly. "Lieutenant Arex, initiate a detailed sensor scan for the captain and Mr. Spock, using Commander Scott's communicator pack as a center point." She directed her words to the pickup again.

"Landing party, prepare to beam up."

"Lieutenant Uhura," Scott countered, "Sulu and I could track down the captain and Mr. Spock from here."

"I'm sorry, Commander Scott," she replied. "You know standard procedure in a case like this—better than I do, I suspect. We've had no response from the missing men. We can't take additional chances without further information on their whereabouts and/or condition."

"We are talking about the *captain*," Scott fumed.

Uhura's voice rose, strained. "I know that, Commander." There was a pause, and when she spoke again her tone was quieter, though no less strained. "We have to follow orders, and regulations. An unresolved situation of this type on a new world, involving an unknown race of still indeterminate potential—and then there's that anomaly. No . . . stand by to beam up, Mr. Scott."

The chief engineer started to reply again. He outranked Uhura, but she was officially in charge as long as he remained on the surface. Besides, she made sense.

"Standing by," he told her tightly. "And—my apologies, lassie. You're right, of course."

If Uhura responded, he didn't hear it, because a faint fog was beginning to obscure vision and perception. The chief became a cluster of chromatically colored particle-wave energy, as did Sulu. The cluster faded, disappeared.

Nothing moved on the shore of the halcyon lake save a few small beetlelike things and one curious quasi lizard, whose attention had been momentarily focused on the incomprehensible apparitions. They were gone now and the creature's blank gaze turned back to the beetles. They were much more interesting, and comprehensible.

"We could rush them, Spock," Kirk surmised as he studied the size and number of aborigines surrounding the captive bn Bem, "but someone might get hurt. I'd rather it wasn't any of them, and I darn sure won't let it be one of us. Their weapons may be crude, but they're effective." He thought a moment. "Maybe we can do it the easy way, simply beam him and then ourselves out of here."

"A facile solution, Captain," concurred Spock.

Kirk brought out his communicator, flipped it open. "Kirk to *Enterprise* . . . Kirk to *Enterprise*."

Silence. He looked down at the compact instrument, listened hard. Even the barely audible low hum which indicated proper activation was absent. Carefully Kirk closed the top, then opened it again. "Kirk to *Enterprise*."

No hum, no reply—so he then began staring at the device. His particular personal communicator had been in his possession for some time. Only . . . this wasn't it.

A glance over at Spock showed that his first officer was examining his own communicator.

"This isn't my communicator, Spock. I know every scratch and smudge on it, and they're all missing from this one."

"Nor is this one mine, Captain," the first officer replied evenly. "Not only is it not mine, it is not anyone's. These are not Federation communicators but clever forgeries. Very clever forgeries." He hefted his experimentally. "Even the weight is correct, though I venture to say they contain anything but operative electronics."

"But it's not possible," Kirk objected dazedly. "This communicator's been with me since we beamed. . . . What now?"

Spock had his phaser out and tried it experimentally. "Our weapons are also substitutes." For confirmation Kirk attempted to rattle a small sapling with his own phaser. Not so much as a leaf was disturbed.

"So our phasers and communicators have been swapped for phonies, Commander bn Bem has run off and gotten himself taken captive by the local primitives, and we've been separated from Scott and Sulu." It was the captain's turn to hike a rarely raised eyebrow. "Mr. Spock, something mighty funny is going on."

His first officer nodded somberly. "I would put it in less colloquial terms, but that is certainly an accurate appraisal of our present circumstances. It would appear that a course of action other than what we originally planned is advisable, until we can discover what is happening, and why."

"Agreed, Spock—except for one thing." He looked back across the log, keeping his profile low. "Commander bn Bem's difficulty seems genuine. Phasers or not, we have to rescue him. If he should be killed while under Federation protection, not to mention ours . . ." The sentence trailed off unfinished.

"Hold it—they're moving."

Both officers watched as the natives began to move off to the west, picking their way easily through the muddy meadows and swampland. Commander bn Bem hiked along readily, making no attempt to slow his captors' progress or leave a trail for would-be rescuers to follow.

Kirk was suddenly struck by the Pandronian's curiously complaisant attitude. "He doesn't act like someone on the verge of being dissected by alien aborigines."

"There's not a great deal he can do, in his present circumstances," Spock suggested.

"I don't buy that, Spock. He ought to be making it difficult for them—struggling, making noise, anything to delay his removal from here. Especially knowing that we were chasing after him. The motives—"

"—of a Pandronian are unknown to us," finished Spock. "In any case, we are badly outnumbered—not to mention being unarmed. We might return to contact Mr. Scott and Lieutenant Sulu. Hopefully *their* phasers and communicators are in working order."

Kirk shook his head. "Can't risk it, Spock. The group is moving. We might never be able to find them again in time to save bn Bem, not in this swamp. And if Scotty's and Sulu's equipment also turned out to be fakes—no, at least now we have the commander in sight.

"Let's stick with them. As long as we stay under cover, we have a chance to surprise them."

Careful and occasionally treacherous pursuit brought them unseen to a vantage point slightly above the natives' destination: a small but neatly arranged village. Several large wooden cages, empty now, reposed at its center. The convoy appeared to be in the process of installing Commander bn Bem in one of the cages.

The thatched huts comprising the village looked competent enough. They were in no way spectacular, not even for primitive architecture. Little in the way of drying sheds, baskets, pottery, or other tools and constructions was visible in the small community. There was nothing to indicate to Kirk that these aliens ranked in the forefront of known primitive races. Spock was obviously dwelling on the same thought.

"These aborigines appear to be in a late primitive state, below urban tribal infrastructure but far above mere nomadic hunters and gatherers. Based on what we have seen thus far, one can deduce that they are at least moderately intelligent and possess a basic language and well-developed social structure. I would assume that a well-developed system of morals, taboos, and traditions is present in the appropriate proportions and degrees of advancement."

He paused, considered a moment before adding, "The standard method of dealing with strangers in such societies may include dismemberment, consumption, or various other unfriendly actions we cannot imagine." He directed a nod toward the now tightly imprisoned Commander bn Bem.

"Judging from the way they have treated the commander so far, I believe we can safely discard such hopeful possibilities as the commander's being treated as a god from the sky, or being adopted into the tribe."

"That's too bad," Kirk murmured. "I think he belongs, somehow. But I agree, Spock." Once again he found himself puzzled by the Pandronian's nonchalant attitude. bn Bem stood calmly in the center of the wooden cage, not pacing or testing the bars or imploring his captors.

"You'd think Commander bn Bem would be able to look at these people and see the same things, yet he's given no indication he finds capture and confinement especially objectionable. If anything, he's behaving as if he's half enjoying it." Kirk shrugged, resigned.

"Well, maybe this is the standard Pandronian way of reacting to capture. As you've pointed out, Spock, we know so little about them." He slid down behind the rotting log in front of them.

"In any case, we can't do anything for him before nightfall. I just hope these aborigines' night vision isn't as well developed as their biceps."

The time remaining until dusk wasn't passed in idleness. Studious searching through the underbrush around the little rise they had encamped on turned up several broken but unrotted sections of tree. These would serve as clubs. A few fist-sized stones coupled with some lengths of native creeper and a little dexterous Vulcan handwork produced a set of efficient-looking bolos.

Thus armed, they waited until the sun had vanished behind the trees in the abrupt manner common to all jungles, before proceeding cautiously down the slope toward the village clearing. Civilization here hadn't reached the elevated plane of intertribal warfare, so Kirk and Spock encountered no posted guards as they entered the outskirts of the village.

Once, something like a cross between a cat and a chartreuse sofa crossed their path. It stared at them with startled red eyes, uttered a single soft yelp like a warped tape, and waddled rapidly out of sight. None of the natives were about. Occasional muffled sounds drifted out from various huts.

"Shhh," Kirk whispered.

"Of course," Spock agreed in near-normal conversational tone. Kirk threw him an exasperated look.

Several moons—one globular, two others of irregular cast—lit the village in ghost light. Eight shapes—the two men and their shadows—moved toward the central cage.

bn Bem noticed their approach and had the grace not to cry out. Silently, Kirk and Spock set to work on the lashings of the cage door.

"Kirk Captain—?"

"Shut up," Kirk ordered, scraping fingers on the crude fiber of the bindings. "We're rescuing you."

"You are interfering with observations."

Even Spock was startled. "*This* is how you observe? By being captured?"

"The opportunities for first-member study are best."

"Assuming the studied don't decide to do a little vivisecting of their own," the first officer observed.

bn Bem adopted a pose of contempt. "Is as *logical* a way as any, Spock Commander."

"Maybe so," put in Kirk, "but I don't think Starfleet would approve. You're being rescued, Commander, whether you like it or not. Come on."

The lashings finally undone, Kirk yanked the door aside. For a minute, as bn Bem stood stolidly in the middle of the cage, the captain was afraid the Pandronian was actually going to resist the rescue. But he finally left the confines of the wooden bars, muttering to himself, using some of the logic he professed to have.

They started for the hill, but were confronted by the unexpected appearance of a light. It did not come from any of the orbiting satellites above. It was small, intense, and wavered slightly.

A second light joined it, then another, and still more. Each light lit a semihumanoid reptilian face, staring into the night. The torches formed a circle around the men. In the flickering light the aborigines' skin took on an ominous blood-red hue.

Kirk took a step backward. As he considered running for it, there was a faint blur before him and something went *ka-thunk* at their feet.

Looking down, he saw the quivering length of a rough-hewn but deadly-looking spear. As a nonverbal means of interspecies communication, it was brutally effective.

"Gentlemen," Kirk observed as the circle of torchbearers moved closer, "I think we're trapped."

"Ineluctably," Spock murmured.

None of them got much sleep the rest of that night, due in large part to the steady noise of saplings being felled around the village and to the steady rumble of their own thoughts. Only Commander bn Bem seemed composed as he studied the native activity.

"Why, Kirk Captain," he exclaimed once, "you are not *observing*."

Kirk thought a few choice thoughts and ignored the Pandronian's sneers. A steady stream of most undiplomatic images eventually lulled him to sleep.

II

When the sun rose again, Commander bn Bem was back in his cage. The village was unchanged, except that the commander now had company. Two cages to his left were also occupied. One imprisoned Kirk; the other held his first officer. A single native guard stood close by, the villagers undoubtedly having decided one was required should any more of the evil strangers suddenly appear.

Kirk had spent futile hours in the predawn darkness testing the lianas which held his cage door closed. But while the aborigines were primitive, they were not stupid. The new knots were far too solid and complex for Kirk to unravel.

A small knife would probably have been enough to saw through the woody lashings. But he didn't have a small knife. Instead, he had a phaser which could carbonize the entire village in a couple of minutes. Only *this* phaser was a phake. It wouldn't incinerate a *Starfleet Technical Manual*.

Kirk doubted that the natives, however lethargic they might otherwise appear concerning their captives, would give him time to gnaw through the bindings with his teeth. He wished he had the tech manual now, anyway. At least it would give him something to read.

Instead, he had to be satisfied with standing morosely at the front of the cage, eyeing the massive guard and muttering to himself.

"How's that, Captain?" Spock queried, overhearing a portion of Kirk's ramblings.

"I was wondering how come we always end up like this, Mr. Spock."

"I assume that's a rhetorical question, Captain."

Kirk sighed, pulled his arms free of the supportive crossbar, and stared through the poles at his first officer. "I was just expressing my astonishment at our ability to get into these situations."

"The common complaint of every human since the dawn of time, I believe," Spock commented philosophically. "It's fate, Captain," he murmured.

Kirk looked surprised. "Fate, Mr. Spock?"

"I think that is the correct term," his first officer said, looking curious rather than uncertain.

Apparently stirred by this incomprehensible alien gabble, the guard strode over to Kirk's cage and poked at the captain with his spear. Kirk jumped back.

"Well, I'm not going to rely on fate to get us out of here." He eyed the guard, who stared back unimpressed. Then Kirk turned a significant expression on Spock.

"Why don't you coax him over to your cage and try a quick Vulcan nerve pinch, Mr. Spock?"

Spock eyed the aborigine warily as the enormous biped turned a neolithic gaze on him. "Captain, I'm *only* a Vulcan. There are limits to what even I can do. It is possible that I could surprise this creature. I could also fail. For one thing, I am unfamiliar with its internal physiology and, specifically, its neural network. Should I guess wrong, it might irritate the creature. I do not believe being taken apart by an aroused native would enhance your own chances of escape, while mine would no longer be in question. Logically, therefore . . ." He shrugged.

Kirk turned his attention back to Commander bn Bem, who had been mercifully silent all morning. "I'm afraid this means we're not going to be able to rescue you at this time, Commander."

His sarcasm was lost on the naturally sarcastic bn Bem. "Good intentions, Captain, are not enough. Planet Pandro will be much displeased. Starfleet Federation told us you were best captain in the fleet. Actions to date deny this."

Kirk had finally had enough. To hell with diplomacy. "Commander bn Bem," he yelled, "you are personally responsible for our present situation!

"You deliberately disobeyed orders, orders given for

your own good, by running off. Your attitude during this entire mission has been extremely abrasive. And I don't know how you did it," he continued dangerously, "but I'm convinced now that you're the one who switched our phasers and communicators for imitations."

"You place too much dependence, Kirk Captain, on phasers and communicators." If Kirk's accusations had dented the Pandronian's insufferable egotism, he gave no sign of it. "Petty instruments. One should rely more on personal resources instead of artificialities."

"Either one of those 'artificialities' could solve our problems right now," grumbled Kirk.

"Is that all?" bn Bem sneered contemptuously. He reached into the pouch at his waist—and produced both phasers and communicators.

"Our phasers!" Kirk exclaimed excitedly. "Throw one—" His excitement was abruptly tempered by realization of what the magical appearance of their devices meant.

"Commander bn Bem," he began carefully, "if you've had those phasers and communicators all this time, why didn't you use them to escape?"

The Pandronian's attitude was that of a parent patiently lecturing a couple of dull-witted children. "You recall will, Kirk Captain, my say that this is best way to observe. As observation is completed, is now time to leave. This One, though, does not demean self by the use of casual violence to accomplish simple goals."

"Oh." Kirk wasn't sure whether he was more fascinated than furious.

"However," the commander concluded, "you may demean yourselves if you wish."

"If we *wish?* Commander bn Bem, I want those phasers and communicators *now*—and for O'Morion's sake, toss them over carefully. They're pretty rugged, but—"

bn Bem waved him off. "Compliance with request is, but is no need to throw. This One must disassemble."

Kirk stared blankly at the Pandronian, the commander's words echoing meaninglessly in his mind, until bn Bem showed what he meant.

Detaching his lower half, the commander split neatly in two and squeezed out through the gaps in the bars, his top half carrying phasers and communicators easily.

Kirk gawked, fascinated, while Spock murmured, "Remarkable." The Pandronian reassembled and handed each of them their instruments. "Truly remarkable. Commander bn Bem is a colony creature. Or perhaps we should begin calling him Commanders bn Bem."

"Commander," Kirk wondered, leaving aside for the moment the question of whether the Pandronian should be addressed in the singular or plural, "if you could split yourself into separate sections, why didn't you escape on your own earlier?"

He set his phaser on low stun and beamed the guard. The huge native slumped, unconscious, on his supporting spear. A careful readjustment of the setting wheel and Kirk was burning away the lashings on his cage, as Spock did likewise to his.

bn Bem watched their efforts idly and continued in the same lecturing tone. "I explained, was not concluded with observating. Also, would deny you the chance to prove your people's value to planet Pandro by rescuing This One from possibly dangerous situation to same."

"For the last time, Commander bn Bem," Kirk declaimed in exasperation, "this is not a laboratory. Not for testing the locals, not for testing us. This is a new, hostile world. And," he added forcefully, "Mr. Spock and I are not your private experimental animals."

"I did not say that," bn Bem objected mildly.

"But you implied it." The Pandronian did not reply. "I have no choice this time," Kirk went on. "Commander, consider yourself under protective custody. We're going to protect you from any further escapades. Mr. Spock, keep an eye on him while I call in. On *all* of him." He flipped open his communicator.

"Kirk to *Enterprise*, Kirk to *Enterprise* . . ."

From his position at the con, Chief Engineer Montgomery Scott leaned forward toward the communications console and asked for the tenth, or possibly hundredth, time, "Lieutenant Arex, have you located them yet?"

The Edoan looked back over a feathery shoulder. "No, sir. It is a large world, filled with many distracting life forms."

Uhura looked up from the main readout screen at Spock's science station. "Mr. Scott! That sensory anomaly—it's expanded to cover the whole northern continent."

"Try more to the south of where we set down," Scott suggested to Arex. "It's possible that—" He blinked, spun in the chair to face Uhura. "What's that, Lieutenant?"

"The sensory distortion—it's covered the entire region. We aren't receiving any information from that area."

"That explains why the detectors are so confused," Arex noted with satisfaction. "I thought they were giving awfully peculiar readings."

Scott left the command chair and walked over to check the readouts at the science station. "That does it, Lieutenant," he said finally. "You couldn't locate the Loch Ness monster through that." His face wrinkled in disgust as he examined the distortion-plagued information.

"These figures look like a regurgitated mass of undigested haggis, and they're about as encouragin'." He looked back at the navigation console. "Nonetheless, Mr. Arex, you've got to keep tryin'."

"Yes, sir."

"Kirk to *Enter*—" The captain paused, studied his communicator. "There's some kind of advanced interference on all channels, Mr. Spock." He looked around nervously. "We're going to have to get out of this village on our own—horizontally, for now. I doubt we'll be able to manage that without being seen."

"I'm afraid I agree, Captain," said Spock, turning to study the still-silent huts.

"Remember, keep your phaser on stun. There are no advanced weapons here, no reason to put a native down permanently. Let's get moving."

They started toward the low rise that he and Spock had descended so hopefully the night before. The concentration of thatched houses was thinner there, but to no avail. As soon as they had emerged from the central clearing, they were spotted by the villagers. The shouting and angry natives reacted to this second escape attempt, as Spock declared sadly, "Most unreasonably."

First one, then a couple, and soon the whole tribe was charging down on them, brandishing spears and clubs and howling deafeningly. The native in the lead, a huge, husky fellow, raised his arm and prepared to hurl one of those thick weapons. His companions started to do likewise.

Apparently the community decision had been made that these strangers were not worth keeping alive any longer.

"Fire," Kirk ordered, at the same time depressing the trigger of his phaser and pointing it at the first aborigine.

Something happened.

His finger froze on the button, unable to depress the trigger the necessary millimeters to fire the weapon. His legs locked in place and his arms were held in an unbreakable yet velvety grasp. Even his eyelids were paralyzed. He tried to blink and couldn't.

Fortunately he wasn't staring at the sun, but he could see Spock nearby, held rigidly in a similar pose in the act of firing his own phaser. Commander bn Bem had been likewise deprived of all mobility.

Around them, the spectrum had gone berserk. He could still see clearly. The charging natives had also been frozen in place, spears poised for flight, clubs held ready to strike—but nothing, nothing looked natural.

Normally brown trees now glowed lambent maroon and sported fluorescent pink foliage. The blue sky overhead had turned a deep green, while the earth underfoot shone orange shot with black. And everything had a hazy, befuzzed edge to it.

Then the Voice sounded.

It was firm, faintly feminine, and hinted at immense power held easily in check. The Voice seemed to originate several centimeters behind Kirk's forehead, and it echoed all around the hollow places within, reverberating gently between his ears.

"No," the Voice instructed, "do not attempt to use your weapons." Kirk experimentally tried to comply and found he could raise his thumb from the trigger. The loosening of control was generalized, enabling him to move his extremities now—fingers, toes, eyes, and mouth.

He utilized the latter to announce unnecessarily, "I'm paralyzed, Mr. Spock."

"We are being held in a new, unique type of force field, Captain," the first officer commented thickly.

"Put away your weapons," the Voice continued. "These are My children. Do not attempt to harm them."

Kirk put aside the question of who was about to harm whom in his desire to learn what was at work here. It was certainly no manifestation of the spear-wielders' minds.

"Who are you?" he asked.

"Who are *you*?" came the reply.

Proceed slowly, he warned himself. This is a powerful, unknown quantity with unknowable motivations. Don't anger it, and don't give anything away.

"I'm Captain James Tiberius Kirk of the Federation cruiser *Enterprise*. On my right is my first officer, Mr. Spock, and on his right, Honorary Commander Ari bn Bem of the Pandro system of worlds."

Kirk received the impression that this honest recounting of names and titles satisfied the Voice.

"Why are you here?" it inquired with what sounded like true curiosity. "Why do you disturb this place?"

"It is part of our mission," Kirk tried to explain, striving to make their assignment sound as innocuous as possible. "We are required to classify this planet. We have to take readings, examine the native population, report the state of—"

The Voice interrupted, not angrily, but annoyed. "What gives you the right to intrude here? This planet was not created for your use. My children are not created to be subjects of your tests. Your weapons, bad things, will be nullified."

Kirk watched the phaser he held simply melt away. He experienced no pain, no sensation of heat—only a slight tingle in his palm after the phaser had completely vanished. The tingling faded rapidly.

"I would say 'nullified' was an understatement, Spock."

Natural color returned without warning. Kirk stumbled, his muscles stiff from being held motionless so long.

Seeing the intruders stumble and the peculiar shiny things disappear from their hands, the natives slowed. They lowered their spears and clubs and clustered tightly around their captives.

"There are times, Mr. Spock," Kirk went on, staring in amazement at his now empty hand, "when I think I should have been a librarian."

"There are those who believe the task of librarian would be equally challenging, Captain," Spock responded as the circle of lowered spears grew denser around them. Sharp points touched the midsections of the three captives. "Though it is undoubtedly less dangerous. . . ."

"The disturbance was temporarily localized, Mr. Scott," Uhura reported from the science console. "I have been able to fix it near what appears to be a village of local native life. It's not far from where you originally set down."

"Never mind the disturbance," Scott muttered, eyeing Arex. "Have you found the captain and Mr. Spock yet?"

"I've located emanations which could be the captain's and Commander Spock's," he explained carefully, with the emphasis on the 'could be.' "But the sensory anomaly has so interfered with our instrumentation that it is impossible to make positive identification at this time."

"Which means—" Uhura began, but Scott cut her off.

" 'Could be' is good enough for me, right now, Lieutenant. Ready a security landing squad. We're going down there with questions and phasers." He rose from the con and headed toward the turbolift.

Kirk, Spock, and bn Bem found themselves secured within the three cages only recently vacated. This time they were surrounded by several guards who looked alert and ugly. Kirk did not enjoy the return to familiar surroundings. Their moment of liberty had been short-lived and short-circuited by a mysterious unseen power which saw fit to side with the antisocial locals. And now they didn't even have the possibility of recovering their phasers or communicators. The former had been melted into nothingness, and the latter were confiscated by their captors.

As might be expected, Commander bn Bem did not improve the situation any. "You've mishandled problem again, Kirk Captain," the Pandronian berated him. "This One judges you not an intelligent captain."

Kirk was almost too discouraged by their failed escape and subsequent recapture to respond. "Commander bn Bem, Mr. Spock and I are here in the first place because we thought you were worth rescuing. Don't misunderstand me. It was to preserve good relations between the Federation and planet Pandro, not out of any overwhelming affection for your person."

"Planet Pandro," bn Bem riposted, "is unconcerned as to fate of This One. Planet Pandro will not have dealings with ineffectual and inferior species. You've failed everything you have attempted. You have not rescued This One and you have not been able to handle local primitives."

At the conclusion of this sneering polemic, seeing

that the guards were temporarily inattentive, the commander literally came apart at the seams.

His head hopped down off his shoulders, moving on
short stumpy legs. His upper torso, headless now,
walked on long arms, while both legs, joined at the top,
slid easily through the bars of the cage. These parts
were followed by the rest of the commander.

The head turned back to call to Kirk and Spock.
"This One wishes you—what is the Federation-Sol
word—luck? Yes, luck. You will require it."

With a contemptuous salute from one of the arms
attached to the upper torso, the components of the
commander scuttled separately into the surrounding
brush.

"Wait! Unlock us—set us free!" Kirk finally gave up
shouting at the unresponsive forest. Meanwhile, the
guards noted the sudden disappearance of one of their
captives, yet again. Much frantic gabbling and gesticulating ensued, after which most of them started off into
the jungle, following the tracks of bn Bem's main legs.
Some shook spears and clubs at the two men still imprisoned, made faces promising dire developments on
their return.

Kirk sympathized with them.

"So much for interspecies loyalty and Pandronian-
Federation friendship," he muttered angrily. "Well,
fine! We're going to get no help from our guest, we
cannot communicate with these natives, and we can't
get through to the ship. What now?"

"Perhaps," Spock mused thoughtfully, "we can regain the attention of the powerful local intelligence and
reason with it."

The aborigines had left the communicators un-
guarded nearby. Spock succeeded in unraveling enough
of one vine to make a small lasso. Kirk watched uneas-
ily, expecting some native to happen along at any moment, while Spock patiently cast and recast the line.

Eventually they regained their communicators. But a
furtive attempt to contact the ship produced the same
results as before—nothing.

Kirk studied the device as if it were capable of producing the miracle they hoped for. "It's worth a try, I suppose." He started to talk, then hesitated. "How do you address something you've never seen and cannot imagine?" He shrugged as Spock regarded him silently.

"Oh, well . . . Kirk to alien intelligence, Kirk to alien intelligence. This is Captain James Kirk calling the controlling intelligence of this world. Answer—respond, please."

He felt something of the fool talking into a communicator directed at thin air. It probably would be as effective to throw his head back and howl at the sky. But using the communicator couldn't hurt.

He continued trying, to continued nonresponse.

"Perhaps an offering of some sort, Captain," suggested Spock.

Kirk eyed his first officer evenly. "Whatever we're dealing with, Mr. Spock, I don't think we can bribe it. Not that we've much to bribe with, but somehow I think it's imperative we be honest with it." He directed his voice to the small pickup and tried again, earnestly.

"Kirk to alien intelligence, Kirk to alien intelligence." He paused, shaking his head. "Good idea, and that's all, Spock."

"Hmmm," the Vulcan murmured. "If we connect our two communicators, we can generate a single high-energy burst, several times the strength a single communicator can put out. That might draw more attention to us." He finished the proposal unwaveringly:

"Doing so will also render both communicators powerless in a very short time."

"Do it," Kirk concurred. "They're useless now anyway, if we can't reach the ship through them."

"The interference could clear later, Captain."

"Yes, but by then our jailers will be back and will take them away from us again. They'll put them way out of reach. Let's take the gamble, Spock."

"Precisely my thoughts, Captain." He extended both hands and arms through the bars of his cage.

Kirk moved over to the side facing Spock's cage. He made a one, two, three gesture with the hand holding the communicator and let it fly with a soft underhand toss. Spock caught it neatly and bent immediately to the task of mating the two instruments.

Ordinarily he could have accomplished the task in a couple of minutes, but the circumstances were not as conducive to such work as were the labs on board the *Enterprise*. Nevertheless, he managed it.

When they were firmly locked together, he tossed the hybrid back to Kirk, who checked the reintegrated circuitry and nodded approval. He switched it on, felt the warmth immediately as the double-powered device began to build toward overload.

"This is Captain James Tiberius Kirk calling the ruling intelligence of this world. Can you hear me? If so, please acknowledge."

He repeated the call over and over, working against the mounting heat in the joined communicators, steadily adjusting the frequency modulator.

"Kirk to entity, Kirk to entity. This is Captain James Tiberius Kirk calling the—"

The wooden bars of the cage turned violet, the ground became orange shot with black, and he found his fingers frozen on the double communicator.

"I am here," the Voice announced gently.

"We apologize for our intrusion," Kirk explained hurriedly. "We didn't realize the true situation here. If we had, we certainly would not have proceeded as we have. If you will permit us, we will leave immediately in our vessel and not return. Nor will others of our kind come.

"If we do not return, then others of our Federation will surely come and you will be troubled no end. Please understand, this is not a threat. They will come not as destroyers, but rather as curious explorers."

There was a long silence during which Kirk discovered that despite his paralysis he could still sweat.

"This is good," the Voice finally decided. Kirk let out a private shout. "Go, then—go now and do not return."

The paralysis vanished. Kirk stretched in relief. "Just one more thing: There's a third member of our group."

"I detect no third intelligence here," the Voice responded, sounding puzzled.

"He, uh, left this immediate area," Kirk hastened to explain.

The Voice ignored him. "You must go. You must not interfere with the natural activities of My children. I will allow you to contact your ship again, but go *now*."

Kirk didn't hesitate. Rapidly he disconnected the two communicators and checked the power leads. "Still functioning—*whew!*" A second sufficed to reset his own communicator on standard ground-to-ship frequency.

"Kirk to *Enterprise*. Kirk to—"

Response was gratifyingly fast. *"Enterprise,"* an excited voice sounded over the little speaker. "Uhura here. Captain, are you all right?"

"Affirmative. Stand by." He looked across at Spock. "We're not leaving without bn Bem. He's still our responsibility, and I won't abandon him here—no matter how much he deserves it. I can't play personalities in this." He returned his attention to the communicator.

"Lieutenant Uhura, beam down a security squad with tricorders set for Pandronian scan."

"Aye, aye, sir. Mr. Scott has already readied one, with phaser cannon."

"Belay that, Lieutenant!" Kirk ordered frantically. "No heavy weapons—just tricorders. Hop to it. Kirk out." He flipped the communicator shut and stuck it back to his waist.

"Cannon or no, the intelligence will still be most displeased, Captain."

"I'll worry about that when I have to, Mr. Spock," replied Kirk firmly. "Our primary concern now is to recover Commander bn Bem, whatever the opposition." He looked toward the center of the village clearing. "Here they come . . ."

Small rainbow whirlwinds began to form before them. Six crew members appeared, five of them clad in security tunics, the sixth in that of the engineering division.

"Captain, Mr. Spock," Scott exclaimed the moment he had fully rematerialized and had time for a look around, "are you all right?" He pulled his phaser, adjusted it, and began burning through the fastenings on the cage door.

"All right now, Scotty," Kirk replied.

The last fiber gave and Kirk was freed. One of the ensigns had performed a similar service for Spock.

"Spread out, staying within sight of each other at all times. You're all familiar with the *Enterprise*'s guest, Commander Ari bn Bem of Pandro?" There were nods and signs of affirmation, several of them embroidered with personal opinion.

"This is a priority assignment," Kirk warned them sternly. "Personal opinions and feelings have no place here. We may encounter hostile native bipeds. Stun only for self-protection, and then only as a last resort.

"Now, let's spread out and try to locate Commander bn Bem. He's split into three individual parts."

"Beggin' pardon, sir," Scott blurted, voicing the general confusion. "Three parts?"

"Commander bn Bem is some kind of colony creature," Kirk explained. "He can operate as a single large individual, as you've seen him, or as three separated segments—maybe more, we don't know." He grinned tightly. "I guarantee you won't confuse part of him for native life."

The group turned and started off toward the section of forest the Pandronian had run into, spreading out as Kirk had directed and working their way through the beginnings of the thickening undergrowth.

As it developed, they got no further than Spock, Kirk, and bn Bem had the previous night.

Captain's admonition or no, when confronted by the sudden appearance of numerous screaming natives three meters tall, all charging toward them waving spears and clubs, none of the security personnel hesitated. Low-power phaser bursts colored the air and several natives dropped, temporarily paralyzed.

The Voice, despite Spock's fears, did not interfere.

The ground remained brown, the leaves green, and their limbs mobile. They continued into the jungle.

It wasn't long before they encountered the main body of warriors. They were returning to the village with a recaptured (and intact) Commander bn Bem in their midst. He was tied like a tiger, every part of his body secured with vines and lianas.

A few phaser bursts were enough to send the rest of the natives running in terror. They left their weapons and fallen comrades and vanished into the trees, leaving a securely bound bn Bem standing alone behind them. Kirk thought the commander looked rather embarrassed.

"We couldn't help it, sir," Scott declared, running over to join Kirk as the captain moved toward the Pandronian. "The crew had to defend themselves."

"Don't worry about it now, Scotty," Kirk reassured him, anxiously studying the sky and the terrain around them. "Let's get our guest and get out of here before we make any real trouble."

bn Bem's head inclined forward and there was a moroseness, a modesty in his tone Kirk had never heard. "Embarrassment results," he declared softly. "This One is shamed. This One has failed in its judgment."

If that was a plea for sympathy, it was wasted on Kirk. "You have endangered all of us by your actions," he chastised the commander, "and you've forced us to interfere with the natives of a world that deserves prime directive protection—not to mention outright quarantine."

The Pandronian struggled to regain some of his former haughtiness. "This One exists by its own standards," he announced, rather lamely.

"Not on my ship, you don't. Not any more. I'll stand for a lot, Commander, but when the Enterprise itself is endangered, diplomacy takes a back seat." He kicked at the dirt and reached for his communicator.

The dirt turned orange and froze in midfall as colorful aberrations swept the landscape and all Kirk's fears were suddenly realized. He fought the paralysis, fought to activate his communicator. If he could just make one shout, relay one order to have them beamed up . . .

But the effort was useless. His finger wouldn't move another millimeter closer to that crucial switch.

There was no fury in the Voice. No spite, no indignation. Kirk had the impression that such petty emotional flavorings were beyond the mind behind the Voice. If it contained any recognizable inflection, it was one of puzzlement.

"You are still here," it announced solemnly. "And you are still interfering." Then it added, without any change in tone, "I am angry."

"We didn't mean to interfere," Kirk explained desperately. "We have our own rules of conduct which forbid intrusion into the affairs of others. We—"

"Then you have not only disobeyed My rules, you have broken your own as well."

"No. We simply could not leave one of our own behind. It is our responsibility to take care of those placed under our protection, just as it's your responsibility to take care of yours.

"We could not leave Commander bn Bem where he could interfere with your"—he hesitated—"children. Would you really want that?" He waited tensely for the response.

"Yes," that rippling voice finally replied, "it is so. You have some wisdom, James Tiberius Kirk. The lost one is found, then?"

"He is found," Kirk admitted. "We will leave."

Another voice sounded—bn Bem's. "This One is greatly distressed. This One has erred. The mission was to judge, and the right of judgment no longer exists. This One must disassemble unity."

"Disassemble?" Kirk started.

"Never again to exist as a cooperation. This unity is defective, insufficient, inadequate, and false. This unit must cease to exist."

Kirk started to protest—certainly a severe reprimand was in order, but as he understood it the Pandronian was contemplating suicide. His personal inclinations were overriden by more powerful concerns. *"No!"*

bn Bem looked around wildly. "What . . . ?"

"Do not destroy yourself."

"But—This One has erred," bn Bem protested. "This One has tried to judge Kirk Captain and Spock Commander, only to be found himself wanting. This One has acted wrongly."

"You may have made a mistake," the Voice declared, without judging the Pandronian's actions in any way, "but if you disassemble you cannot learn from your error. Errors demand recognition. They also demand nonrepetition. If you disassemble, you will not be able to never repeat your mistake."

Spock admired the logic of it while bn Bem argued uncertainly. "And you—you do not demand punishment, for the breaking of your laws?"

Kirk was ready to scream; was bn Bem trying to get them *all* disassembled? He needn't have worried. He was underestimating their observer.

"Punishment?" Now the puzzlement was unmistakable. "What is punishment?"

"Revenge."

"Revenge? Intelligent beings require no revenge. Punishment is necessary only where learning cannot occur without it. You are behind such things as I am above it. My children here are different. That is why you must leave, so as not to corrupt their development with such obscene concepts as punishment and revenge."

The last comment was uttered with an inflection of contempt so strong it made Kirk momentarily dizzy.

"I am humbled," was all bn Bem managed to whisper.

Suddenly Kirk found that his own anger at bn Bem had become a source of embarrassment. "We'll be on our way now, if we may," he asked humbly.

"Yes. Go now . . ."

Natural coloration returned to the jungle and Kirk regained control of his body. For a long moment he studied the landscape, but saw only trees and vines, heard only the sounds of bird-things and shy crawlers. There was the rustle of a breeze. Nothing more.

He took out his communicator, addressed it slowly. "Kirk to *Enterprise*. Beam us up . . ."

bn Bem was with him as the captain resumed his position at the con. "Stand by to break orbit."

Spock was back at the library station, awaiting instructions. "Mr. Spock, classify this planet, Delta Theta Three, as being under strict Federation quarantine from this stardate forward. Said quarantine subject to Starfleet review of the official report of this mission. Under no circumstances is any vessel to approach this world."

"A restriction planet Pandro will also respect," bn Bem declared helpfully.

"I compliment you both on a wise decision, gentlemen," said Spock, working to prepare the necessary documentation.

"It's necessary for them as well as for us, Spock," Kirk explained.

Spock nodded, turned his gaze to the main viewscreen. It displayed a wide-sensor picture of the planet in question, still rotating demurely below them, giving no hint of the extraordinary alien intelligence inhabiting it.

"It is fascinating, Captain. A highly advanced alien entity using this system as a laboratory for guiding another people to racial maturity. Almost a god, you might say."

"Such comparisons are as meaningless as they are farfetched, Mr. Spock. By contrast to the ruling mind of Delta Theta Three, we are all children."

"In This One's case," bn Bem mumbled with becoming humility, "is still an eggling."

Kirk looked gratified. If, despite all the trouble, this expedition had taught the Pandronian a little modesty, then it was worth all they'd been through.

"Take us out of orbit, Mr. Sulu. It's time to—"

Uhura broke in with an exclamation of surprise. "Captain, I'm picking up a transmission from the surface."

"Put it through the bridge speakers, Lieutenant."

Kirk, Spock, and bn Bem recognized that wizened,

maternal voice, which rippled and heaved with vast sighs like some midocean wave:

"Go in peace. Go in peace, children. You have learned much, though you have much left to learn. Be proud and—someday, perhaps—return."

That was the tantalizing bequest they bore with them as, at warp four, the *Enterprise* left the system of the sun Delta Theta.

That was a promise worth carrying home. . . .

III

Kirk and Spock remained affected by their contact with the extraordinary intelligence experimenting on Delta Theta Three, only in their case the effects didn't show. The opposite was true of Commander Ari bn Bem.

In contrast to the first part of the voyage, the commander had turned into a model passenger. His demeanor as they traveled toward Starfleet Science Station 24 was downright subdued.

Previously his interest in Federation procedures and operations had run from nonexistent to outright disdain. Following the humbling experience on Delta Theta Three, he exhibited a powerful desire to use the limited time remaining to him to learn all he could about the methods of Federation survey, navigation, research, and other exploratory techniques. So furiously did he plunge into his new studies that Kirk feared for his health. The commander refused to slow down, however.

"Have wasted much time already, Kirk Captain," bn Bem told him in response to Kirk's expressions of concern. "This One's ignorance must be assuaged. Cost to body self is negligible in comparison."

bn Bem's prior intransigence manifested itself now and then, but only when the material he wished to absorb wasn't instantly available, or when he chose to dispute a bit of science or procedure. So hard did he question various technicians that they almost wished they were again victims of the Pandronian's contempt instead of his voracious desire to learn.

It had been Kirk's intention to leave the commander at Science Station 24. According to the captain's original orders from Starfleet Command, the commander would remain at the station for a month, intensively researching Federation analytic methodology until a Pandronian ship arrived to take him home.

But Kirk was not to lose bn Bem's company as soon as he thought.

"I have contact with Science Station Twenty-four, Captain," Uhura announced. "They have an urgent message."

"Classified?" Kirk asked discreetly, with a glance at the science station, where bn Bem was engaged in earnest discussion with Spock.

Uhura checked her instrumentation. "It doesn't appear to be, Captain."

"Very well, Lieutenant. Put it on the screen." Kirk swiveled the command chair as Uhura moved to comply. A brief burst of static and the viewscreen produced a portrait.

The face of Lieutenant Commander Kunjolly stared back at him. Long white sideburns looking like puffs of steel wool flared out from skin the hue of dark chocolate. In an age of scientific miracles, the station commander's smooth pate was a glaring anomaly.

"Captain Kirk," the slightly high-pitched voice offered in greeting. "Good to see you again."

"Hello, Monty," a smiling Kirk replied. "Nice to see you, too. I have some good news for you." It would be considered more than good, he reflected, when the no doubt apprehensive station staff learned of their incipient guest's transformation.

"And I have some puzzling news," Kunjolly riposted, "though not for you. But go ahead and tell me yours first."

Kirk looked uncertainly at the screen. "All right."

He glanced over at the science station. The conversation between bn Bem and Spock had grown lively.

"Your assigned visitor had an experience at our final survey stop which seems to have modified the inherent irascibility of his kind. I don't know how familiar you are with the Pandronians, but you'll be glad to know that this one's become almost charming."

Kunjolly grinned back at him. "That's very gratifying to learn, Captain." The grin turned to a concerned frown. "Though I wonder if we'll be enjoying his company for long."

Kirk's puzzlement grew. "What are you talking about, Monty?" Visions of having to play host to even a reformed bn Bem rose in his mind.

The station commander shuffled some papers out of Kirk's view, then looked back into the pickup. "I'm holding a sealed message for your Pandronian VIP, Captain, beamed straight to us from his homeworld of Pandro."

"For me a message?" came a startled query. Apparently bn Bem hadn't been as totally absorbed in his conversation with Spock as Kirk had thought. Now he ambled over to stare at the screen, then down at Kirk.

"What means this, Kirk Captain?"

"I was hoping you could tell me, Commander."

"This One is expecting no sealed messages from home," bn Bem declared openly. "This One is thoroughly puzzled."

"You've no idea what the message is?"

"None more than you, Kirk Captain."

"Oh, and something else, Captain Kirk."

Kirk glanced back up at the screen. "What is it, Monty?"

The station commander looked to his left. "I have additional orders for the *Enterprise* from Starfleet Command. They read as follows:

" 'The *Enterprise* is hereby directed to provide, pursuant to Federation law and naval restrictions, all services requested by Pandronian representative Commander Ari bn Bem subsequent to his receipt of important message to him from his government.' "

"That's all very irregular," Kirk observed, a mite testily. "Why wasn't the message sent directly to us? It could have reached us several days ago."

"The Federation orders came through only this morning, stationtime, Captain Kirk. As for the Pandronian message, there wouldn't have been any point in sending it to you."

"Why not?" Kirk wanted to know.

"It was stated explicitly in English accompanying the Pandronian that delivery of the message was to await complementary orders from Starfleet—the one that came through this morning.

"Besides, it's all in Pandronian code. I wouldn't like to try transcribing it for rebroadcast. No one here has any clue as to the contents of the message."

"Someone at Starfleet must, Captain," Spock put in, "if they acceded so readily to the Pandronian request."

"Not necessarily, Spock," Kirk mused thoughtfully. "The Pandronians might have made a request for unspecified aid. Starfleet wants Pandro as an ally badly enough that they might have promised our help without knowing the specifics of what that help is wanted for."

"That is possible, Captain," Spock conceded.

"Very well. The sooner we dock in, the faster we'll find out what this is all about." He snapped directions to those manning the con. "Mr. Sulu, Mr. Arex, bring us into Station Twenty-four. Gently, if you please." His attention returned to the screen.

"We should be in your office in a little while, Monty. I expect you're as curious to know the nature of that message from Pandro as we are."

"I am, Captain Kirk. However, the orders from Starfleet are all-inclusive, which means that Commander bn Bem need not apprise us of his message's contents."

"I know," Kirk admitted, trying not to let his worry show. "*Enterprise* out."

"Station Twenty-four out," a solemn Kunjolly acknowledged, closing the transmission.

"Well, Commander," Kirk began, facing bn Bem, "still no idea of what's going on?"

"Not ever before have I heard of such a thing, Kirk

Captain," the Pandronian replied. He seemed genuinely concerned. Reflecting his nervousness, his head shifted from side to side on his shoulders.

Even though he knew that a Pandronian could separate his body into at least three major sections—each one capable of independent motility—Kirk still found it unnerving to see the commander adjust his structure so casually.

"It must be important, Captain," insisted Spock from his position at the science station. "By requesting such extreme assistance from Starfleet, the Pandronians are jeopardizing their neutrality. That is a great deal to risk merely to speed the commander on his way. Obviously, his presence is desired for some emergency so severe that they cannot wait for one of their own ships to come and pick him up."

"Makes sense, Mr. Spock," the captain agreed. From what he knew of Pandro, which was little, Kirk found the entire situation unlikely. Something had worried the Pandronian government enough for them to modify their fierce independence. That was all to the Federation's good, but not necessarily to that of his ship.

Science Station 24 consisted of a central hub in the shape of a slowly turning disk from which the multiple spokes of connector passageways protruded. Various-shaped modular stations bulged at the terminus of each long pressurized corridor; spheres, cubes, ellipsoids, and combinations of these and other forms held laboratories and living quarters, the whole station a hallucinant's vision of an exploded popcorn ball.

Each module housed a different function, from complete laboratories dedicated to the study of zero-g biology to long tubular structures filled with facilities for examining the movement of subatomic particles.

One of the longer spokes ended in a simple large airlock. No other modules were placed near it. Even so, it was a delicate maneuver on Sulu's part to align the *Enterprise* properly with the station docking port. The simple spoke provided none of the navigational aids of a completely self-enclosed Starfleet station dock, but those weren't required here. Only supply ships and occasional ships like the *Enterprise* on special missions stopped at the isolated research stations. Elaborate facilities would have been wasted.

Gravity increased to near normal as the turbolift carried Kirk, Spock, and Commander Ari bn Bem down the long pressurized shaft toward the central station hub. From the central turbolift depot, where cargo and passenger lifts transported supplies and personnel to the many distant lab modules, it was a short walk to the outer offices of the station commandant, Lieutenant Commander Kunjolly. An ensign greeted them and after a short conversation via intercom, directed them to the inner sanctum.

"Good to see you again, Captain Kirk," Kunjolly exclaimed as the three entered. He left his desk to shake Kirk's hand, then repeated the formality with the *Enterprise*'s first officer. "And you, Mr. Spock."

"Dr. Kunjolly," the science officer said by way of return, using a warmer title than the station chief's military one. Spock was anxious to learn the nature of Kunjolly's extraordinary message for bn Bem, and the sooner formalities, however pleasant, were over, the better he would like it.

Spock's concern was echoed by the tall blue form alongside him. "Anxiousness This One expresses to observe message," stammered bn Bem hurriedly.

"I understand," Kunjolly declared. Returning to his seat behind the big desk, he passed a palm over its left side. There was a soft beep, duplicated by a second beep as his hand crossed over the spot once again.

A panel flipped open behind the desk. All three guests watched as the station commandant used an electronic key to open a locked drawer. After removing a tiny metal cube he relocked the drawer and pressed a hidden button. A three-panel viewer common to conference rooms on the *Enterprise* popped up in the center of the desk. Kunjolly inserted the message cube properly and hit still another switch.

Kirk and Spock stared expectantly at the tripartite screen as it lit up, but the flow of information which raced across was disappointingly incomprehensible. Not that either man had anticipated understanding the Pandronian message, but Kirk had half hoped he could make something out of the communication.

The complex cryptography proved totally alien, though, as alien as the Pandronians themselves. While Kirk waited impatiently, Commander bn Bem avidly examined the steady stream of information. Occasionally the Pandronian would produce a low gurgling noise, sounding like a faulty water pipe, but otherwise he remained silent as he studied the message. At the conclusion of the message, bn Bem let out a startling yelp, his eyes rolled over, and he collapsed to the floor.

"Commander bn Bem!" Kirk shouted, rushing to kneel above the motionless form. Kunjolly hurried around from behind his desk, and Spock also bent over the prone Pandronian. The commander's eyes remained shut and his upper torso appeared to be shivering slightly.

Kirk put out a hand toward one shoulder, intending to give the body a gentle shake, and abruptly hesitated.

"Mr. Spock, how much do we know of Pandronian physiology?"

"Practically nothing, Captain."

Kirk's hand drew back.

Kunjolly's hands had tightened into worried fists. "There must have been something powerful in that message. It appears to have induced a fatal shock."

"No matter the cause," Spock noted grimly. "If he dies here, aboard a Federation outpost while under Federation protection, we will be blamed. Not for inducing the shock—that is surely the fault of the message—but for not knowing how to cure its effects. Pandronian-Federation relations will suffer."

Kirk noticed that the shivering continued. "He's not dead—not yet, anyway. Monty, get in touch with your medical personnel. Mr. Spock, contact Dr. McCoy, explain what's happened, and have him rush down here. Perhaps working together we can—"

Spock put up a hand for silence. "Just a moment, Captain, Dr. Kunjolly." The station commandant paused at his desk, one hand ready to activate the intercom there.

Kirk stared in fascination. The body of the unconscious Pandronian was coming apart. First the lower torso slithered away from the commander's stomach. The upper torso, moving on mobile arms, detached itself at the lower part of the neck. Both lower and upper body sections moved independently to take up positions on either side of the limp head.

Tiny cilia extending from the upper part of the hips commenced a feathery caress of the face while the two hands massaged the back of the skull, which raised up slightly on cilia of its own to provide easy access for the arms.

Kirk stared openmouthed at the nightmare scene being played out before them. "The Pandronian form," Spock commented quietly, "appears capable of taking care of itself under circumstances which would leave a human—or Vulcan—relatively helpless."

As if to confirm further the first officer's speculation, Commander bn Bem's eyes blinked open seconds later. Still moving on neck cilia, the now-alert head adjusted itself on the floor. Rushing about like a family of varmints scurrying to flee an owl, the remaining sections of the commander's body reattached themselves at neck and stomach.

bn Bem placed both hands on the floor and sat up, staring at the stupefied onlookers with a puzzled expression. "This One fainted at import of message, Kirk Captain. Something the matter is?"

"Uh, you fell down without warning. We thought you needed assistance."

bn Bem got to his feet, a touch of his natural aloofness reasserting itself. "Is not to worry. Natural superiority of Pandronian lifeform assures self-care in such matters." He moved to the desk, addressed a still-dazed Kunjolly. The station commandant, Kirk reminded himself, had not seen the startling Pandronian separate-but-equal performance before today.

"Import of message overwhelmed This One temporarily. Must run through again, please."

"What?" muttered Kunjolly, in the voice of a man emerging from a dream.

"Must see again the message." bn Bem gestured at the blank triple screen.

"Yes . . . of course." The station commandant regained his composure and pushed the appropriate button. Once more the coded Pandronian message splashed its cryptic contents across the desk screens.

Spock chose the moment to whisper to Kirk, "A most interesting display, Captain, on the commander's part. Apparently the shock of the message only incapacitated the brain, leaving the rest of the body free to work at restoring consciousness. A useful function for an intelligent being to have. The advantages would apply to a host of diseases—the problems of hangover, for example."

"True," agreed Kirk readily. "I can see where—" He paused, gaped at his first officer. "Now, why would a nonimbibing Vulcan be interested in hangover remedies, Mr. Spock?"

"While not subject to such a primitive malady, Captain, I can still appreciate the luxury of a physiology which keeps the rest of the body from suffering for the transgressions of a poorly functioning brain."

Kirk was about to reply when he was interrupted by a series of shouts and yelps from Commander bn Bem. The Pandronian was twisting his hands about one another in an unfamiliar fashion while shaking his head from side to side. On occasion as the commander gave vent to his emotions his head would lift up slightly on its motile cilia and run back and forth on his shoulders, sometimes turning complete circles. This was an upsetting sight even to one who by now should be inured to the unique abilities of the Pandronian form.

"Oh, woe! Oh, incomprehensibility! Oh, abomination most sublime!" bn Bem turned eyes filled with disbelief on Kirk. "Something that cannot be imagined has happened."

Kirk noted that the screens were blank once again. The message had run its course for the second time.

He wondered how much of this naked emoting was for his benefit, in anticipation of a request yet to come.

At least the commander's head had ceased its gyrations and had seen fit to sit in normal head-fashion solidly on bn Bem's shoulders. For this Kirk was thankful. "Is there something we can do to help?" he asked, knowing full well that the Pandronian government had already made that request of Starfleet Command, albeit in a generalized form.

"Is," acknowledged bn Bem tersely. "Must go This One with you to planet Pandro immediately."

"With us?" Kirk exclaimed, his eyebrows suddenly matching Spock's for altitude.

"That explains the orders, Captain," Spock pointed out.

"Yes, to go immediately all of us," the excited Pandronian insisted. "No delay to be brooked." He brushed past Kirk and Spock as he headed for the outside corridor leading toward the central station hub. "Without pause follow now, Kirk Captain. Of the essence is time."

"But we——" Too late; the commander was gone, presumably on his way back to the *Enterprise*.

Kirk took a deep breath, turned back to a dumbfounded Kunjolly.

"I'd like to see those Starfleet orders for myself, Monty."

"Of course, Captain," the station commandant replied understandingly. Reaching into his desk, he withdrew another cube, replaced the Pandronian message cube with it, and activated the playback.

This time the triple screen bloomed with the face and upper body of a Starfleet admiral. A second human hovered in the background of the recording. Kirk didn't recognize the nonspeaker's face, but the trim uniform of the Federation Diplomatic Corps was unmistakable. Both he and Spock listened as the verbal orders played through. It was quiet in the office for a long moment after the communiqué ceased.

"But surely, Monty," Kirk argued out loud, "rendering services can't mean that Commander bn Bem is permitted to commandeer the *Enterprise* for his own private transportation."

Kunjolly looked thoughtful, then ventured almost apologetically, "What are your next stated orders, Captain?"

"Actually, we don't have any," Kirk told him. "On dropping off Commander bn Bem here we were supposed to"—his voice sank—"await new directives from Starfleet."

"In the absence of additional orders or specifics, the message appears inarguable, Captain," Spock finally mused aloud. "We are to provide whatever services Commander bn Bem requires, while keeping within Federation law. The commander desires to go directly to Pandro, therefore we must take him there.

"I confess I too have mixed feelings about traveling to the world which developed those attitudes the commander espoused prior to our experiences on Delta Theta Three, but naturally we cannot allow personal opinions to interfere with the Starfleet directive."

"Naturally," Kirk concurred. "Though just this once I wish that—" He stopped, frowning. "Spock, we don't know why the commander has to go to Pandro so quickly. Could it violate Federation and Starfleet law if he fails to tell us?"

"Unfortunately," Spock responded, "I am afraid that because our orders were so general in scope, he need not. But considering his altered attitude, I have grounds to believe he will."

"Good-bye, Monty," Kirk said quickly. "It looks as if you'll have to wait a while longer to entertain a Pandronian representative."

"From what I've heard and seen, Captain," the station commandant replied, "I don't think the delay will upset too many of my associates."

After rushing for the turbolift depot, Kirk and Spock had to wait around for an empty capsule. In his haste to return to the *Enterprise*, a frantic Commander bn Bem had taken the last one by himself.

"I hope," Kirk noted with wry amusement, "he has

the decency to wait for us to return before leaving. I wouldn't put it past him to try to order the *Enterprise* about on his own!"

IV

The Pandronian commander didn't go quite that far, but his impatience was unmistakable to Kirk when he walked onto the ship's bridge.

"Is in greatest hurry to depart, Kirk Captain," bn Bem rattled off at top speed, accompanied by much waving of hands and rolling of eyes. At least the eyes remained in place in his head, Kirk mused gratefully. "Is of the urgency utmost to proceed to Pandro at maximum velocity."

"Just try to take it easy, Commander," Kirk advised the apoplectic Pandronian as both he and Spock resumed their stations. "We'll get you there as fast as is practicable."

"Not to delay," bn Bem advised him, his voice assuming a warning tone. "Is best for all to remember the delicate nature of present negotiations between planet Pandro and Federation, not to mention Pandro and Klingon Empire."

"Don't threaten me, Commander," Kirk told him quietly. "I have my orders, which instruct me to take you home if that is your wish. I'll carry those orders out." His voice rose ever so slightly: "But threats from you or anyone else won't slow me or speed me in doing so."

"Slow you or speed you in doing what, Jim?" another voice inquired.

Kirk glanced over a shoulder, saw that McCoy had entered the bridge. "In going to Pandro, Bones."

McCoy's body, unlike Commander bn Bem's, was incapable of separating into three independent parts. The expression on the good doctor's face as he heard Kirk's announcement, however, seemed to suggest that he felt ready to give it a try. His gaze traveled incredulously from Kirk to the phlegmatic bn Bem, then back to Kirk again.

"Pandro! I thought we were going to leave this—going to leave Commander bn Bem here at the station, then proceed on new orders."

"Those *are* our new orders, Bones, as interpreted by Mr. Spock and myself. We are to render unto bn Bem whatever bn Bem requires. Right now he requires that we get him to Pandro pronto."

"But why, Jim? Why us? Why not a Pandronian vessel?"

"Yes, why the unusual haste, Commander?" asked Spock from the science station.

"Insensitive beings!" bn Bem raged, a touch of his former personality reasserting itself. "Unfeeling ones! Explanations to demand while sacrilege occurs!"

Still fuming at the incomprehensible insult caused by Spock's simple question, the commander stalked off the bridge.

McCoy stared after the fuming alien until the turbolift doors had closed behind him, then glanced sardonically back to Kirk. "Well, now that everything's been made clear . . ."

"Do not be too harsh on our guest, Doctor," advised an ever considerate Spock. "From what we now know of his psychology I have to guess that his fury is motivated not by hostility but by some real atrocity which has taken place on his homeworld. I believe that if we do not press him for information now, he will inform us of the cause of his anguish before we arrive at Pandro."

For a long while it didn't look as if the first officer's prediction would come to pass. Commander bn Bem remained secluded in his cabin, having his meals sent in and refusing to have anything whatsoever to do with anyone. All invitations to emerge were met with a stony silence, broken occasionally by gruff mutters in Pandronian which sounded vaguely like cursing.

All that changed of necessity when the *Enterprise* eventually entered orbit around Pandro and the transporter room was prepared to beam them down. Or so Kirk thought as he, Spock, and McCoy stood waiting in the chamber for the commander to appear.

"Surely, Jim," a still disbelieving McCoy murmured, "we're not going to beam down to a world possibly populated by arrogant megalomaniacs without having the slightest idea of what we're letting ourselves in for?"

"Don't worry, Bones. We're going to stay right here until I get some kind of explanation out of bn Bem."

"If you recall the wording of our orders from Starfleet, Captain . . ." Spock put in by way of gentle reminder.

"I recall the wording perfectly, Spock. We are to render service to Commander bn Bem as he requires."

When it became clear that the captain had nothing to add, Spock pressed on. "Would you still refuse him beam-down then, Captain, if he continues to refuse information?"

Kirk smiled knowingly. "Of course not, Spock. As you just noted, I couldn't do that without violating our orders. But I'm betting that bn Bem, this close to home, won't want to chance that."

Several minutes passed in idle speculation among the officers as to the cause of the Pandronian commander's extraordinary summons home. No one had produced a likely explanation by the time the subject of their conversation arrived.

Spock and McCoy followed Kirk into the Transporter Chamber, while Commander bn Bem exercised his newly won knowledge by moving to the transporter console where he instructed Chief Scott on beam-down coordinates. Scott had to admit to himself that the Pandronian had done his homework; the coordinates were precise and neatly translated from Pandronian navigational terms.

The commander moved rapidly then to take up a position alongside the three waiting officers. Kirk nodded toward the console.

"Stand by to energize, Mr. Scott."

"Standin' by, sir," replied the chief engineer.

Kirk waited a couple of seconds for effect before he

turned to stare hard at the Pandronian. "All right, Commander bn Bem. We've brought you this far unquestioningly, but we're not beaming down until I find out what we're likely to encounter. What was that message you received all about?"

"At once to beam down!" the commander retorted angrily. "At once to waste no more time. Is for you to remember orders that—"

Kirk was shaking his head slowly. "Sorry, *that* won't work any more, Commander. Our orders directed us to render you whatever service you required in accordance with Federation law and regulations. For us to beam down ignorant of surface conditions which might prove hazardous to Federation personnel—ourselves—would be in violation of those laws." bn Bem said nothing, but continued to stare belligerently at Kirk.

"Well," Kirk finally prompted the Pandronian, "which'll it be? Do we get some information, or do we sit here until I can get clarification from Starfleet headquarters? And unless Pandronian bureaucracy is astonishingly more efficient than its Federation counterparts, you know how much time *that* will take."

Commander bn Bem's gaze turned toward the deck and he was obviously struggling to control himself. "Is time for This One to have patience," he mumbled. "Is better to be pleasant with misunderstanders."

Eventually he looked up and explained tersely, "You will comprehend full meaning not, but has been *stolen* the Tam Paupa." His enunciation of "stolen" conveyed a sense of intense disgust and disbelief, evident to every listener on the bridge despite their differences in species.

"The Tam Paupa?" Kirk repeated, wrestling with the supple but guttural pronunciation. "I'm afraid we don't know what that is, Commander bn Bem."

The Pandronian looked exasperated. "Did I say not you would not understand? This One endeavors to elucidate.

"Has been worn well Tam Paupa by every ruler of United Planet Pandro for"—he hesitated briefly—"for twelve thousand of your years. To understand importance of Tam Paupa you must realize, hard though it be, Kirk Captain, that on rare occasions we Pandronians can be slightly testy, and argumentative even."

"Oh, we couldn't possibly think of you that way," McCoy chirped in sarcastically, "but if you say it's true, I suppose we'll have to believe you—hard though it be."

"Take it easy, Bones," Kirk whispered to the doctor, but McCoy's sarcasm was apparently lost on the worried Pandronian.

"Is the wearing of Tam Paupa," bn Bem continued, "which gives elected premier of Pandro the ability to govern fairly and without animosity toward others. Is talent recognized and honored by all Pandronians. Wearer of Tam Paupa never accused of injustices or favoritisms. This has preserved our civilization, Kirk Captain, has permitted Pandro to reach present heights. To imagine government without Tam Paupa not possible.

"An example This One gives. Sixteen hundred of your years ago, was stolen from premier, Tam Paupa. Chaos and civil wars resulting took three hundred years to recover from. That this again should happen is unthinkable." He looked simultaneously revolted and downcast. "Yet happen it has."

"I think I understand, Commander," Kirk responded sympathetically as bn Bem turned away to hide his emotions.

Kirk whispered to the nearby Spock and McCoy, "This Tam Paupa is some sort of crown or other device that somehow enhances the decision-making ability of the elected Pandronian leader while assuring the general populace of his continued impartiality. I'd like to have a look at the mechanism."

"So would I, Captain," Spock agreed readily. "Such a device, if it truly does what the commander says it does, could benefit others besides the Pandronians."

"And now it's been stolen," added McCoy. "Last time it caused three centuries of civil war." He whistled softly. "No wonder the Pandronians are panicked."

"It would appear, Captain," the first officer went on, "that we have been presented a chance to solidify the Federation's position vis-à-vis formal interstellar relations."

"You mean do more than just transport the commander home, as our orders indicate?" Kirk said. Spock nodded slowly and Kirk considered uncertainly. "I don't know, Spock. We know so little about Pandro. What little we do know seems to point to a highly developed society fighting to survive on a primitive world."

"No more time to waste on murmurings idle," a pleading bn Bem interrupted them. "Now to rush-hurry-quick with transporting."

Devoid of any reason to stall further, Kirk gave his assent. The three officers resumed their positions prior to transporting as Kirk faced the console.

"You can energize, Mr. Scott."

"Aye, Captain," the chief engineer acknowledged from behind the console. "I dinna know where these coordinates will set you down. I hope the commander knows what he's doin'."

Kirk recalled the last time they'd set down on a world after bn Bem had programmed the transporter. He uncomfortably remembered rematerializing several meters above open water. But he said nothing, mentally seconding Scotty's wish.

His first impression was that he had materialized at the point of a gun. That was his thought as he stared at the tubular-shaped, lethal-looking instrument a grim-faced and very blue Pandronian was pointing directly at his chest. Glancing around, he saw that the little group was surrounded by similarly armed, equally determined Pandronians.

"What's this all about, bn Bem?" McCoy asked, fighting to keep his anger in check.

"An explanation would certainly seem to be in order, Commander," Spock added more calmly. But he didn't take his eyes off the Pandronian covering him.

"A precaution only, gentlemen," the commander assured them. He spoke to the guards in his own language. Abruptly the weapons went vertical and the intimidating circle turned into an escort of honor.

"This way, please," bn Bem indicated. Kirk, Spock, and McCoy followed the commander at a rapid pace down a high-ceilinged, triangular-shaped corridor, their former captors flanking them on either side.

"I still do not understand," Spock persisted.

"Is sad to admit, Spock Commander," bn Bem proceeded to explain, "but are somewhat paranoid we Pandronians where other races are concerned. As was This One until enlightening experience on Delta Theta Three."

Privately Kirk felt that describing Pandronians as "somewhat paranoid" severely understated their state of mind, but it would have been undiplomatic to argue the point.

They turned several bends in the corridor as Spock wondered aloud, "How did the guards know where we were going to materialize, Commander? You had no contact with the surface prior to our beaming down."

"Oh, is standard landing coordinates for all un-Pandronian visitors," bn Bem told them. "Detectors in chamber sense utilization of various transporter fields and so are alerted the guards."

That satisfied the first officer. It also inspired Kirk to reflect on the fact that the Pandronians were an advanced people whose friendship was well worth cultivating even if their personalities could be somewhat disagreeable.

It also caused him to wonder how the Tam Paupa could have been stolen, since the Pandronians were clearly very security-minded.

A final bend in the corridor and they came up against a closed and guarded door. Commander bn Bem spoke to the two neatly uniformed guards standing before it, and the little party was admitted instantly.

The room they entered was roughly circular in shape. A broad window across the floor showed that they were at least thirty meters above the surface of Pandro. A view of the disjointed Pandronian architecture of the capital city of Tendrazin was visible through the transparent acrylic. Green trees and fuzzy growths of all kinds brightened the cityscape, as would be expected on a world which was primarily savanna and jungle.

The chamber itself was domed, the roof blending into walls of blue, green, and yellow tile. Light filled the room, courtesy of the vast oval skylight above. Where the skylight met the walls, the glass or plastic was composed of multihued mosaics depicting scenes from Pandronian history.

From various points above, globular lamps hung by long thin tubes to provide additional illumination. Scroll cases and sealed cabinets of a wood like oiled cherry lined the walls, alternating with closed doors.

A large half-moon desk of darker wood rested on a raised dais at the far end of the impressive chamber, backed by the sweeping window. Several rows of curved, thickly padded benches formed concentric arcs before it, the seats adjusted to accommodate the Pandronian physique.

"This is the innermost *Pthad*," bn Bem explained with a touch of pride in his voice, "the seat of our government. Here meet the integrals of the high council to determine policy for all Pandro."

McCoy's attention was focused not on the sumptuous appointments or the view of the city beyond, but on something sandwiched between two nearby cabinets.

"What's that?"

bn Bem glanced in the direction indicated by the doctor. "Is one of the premier's favorite pets."

McCoy strolled over to the large rectangular cage. It was formed of narrow slats of some bright gray metal. Its floor was covered with what appeared to be a mixture of natural growth and dry wood shavings.

Resting in the center of the cage floor lay an animal. It had a plump round body covered with bristly brown fur about a centimeter in length. Seven pairs of legs protruded from seven clearly defined segments. A double tail tipped one end while a tiny ball of a head indicated the other. A single eye glared from its center, with nostrils set to either side and a mouth both above and below the eye.

At the moment, the apparition was munching sedately on some leaves or green paper—Kirk couldn't decide which. It peered up at the onlookers, its single blue eye blinking placidly.

"Not a very cuddly-looking pet," McCoy commented with distaste.

"The *diccob* is amusing, though," countered bn Bem, "and responsive. Watch."

Clapping his hands twice, the commander let out a low-pitched whistle. Immediately the *diccob* eyed him—and went all to pieces. Literally.

Eight sections, including the head, fell away from each other and performed a little scurrying dance, weaving about themselves. As if on cue, they unexpectedly came together. Only now the *diccob* stood erect, a bipedal form. Two segments served as legs, three as a body above, with a pair for arms topped by the head. The twin tail had also divided itself, and each tail formed a gripping tentacle at the terminus of each arm.

Apparently as content in this new shape as in its former one, the *diccob* returned to its eating. Kirk wondered at the marvels of adaptive internal physiology which permitted such rapid dissolution and reforming without any evident harm or loss of efficiency to the animal.

"Amusing, is not?" bn Bem inquired.

" 'Fascinating' would be a better term," a thoroughly engrossed Spock suggested. "Is it capable of assuming more than two forms?"

"Watch," was all the commander said. Under his hand and voice directions, the *diccob* executed several more collapses and reassemblies, concluding with a fully circular shape which rolled spiritedly around the cage like an animated wheel, the cyclopean head tucked safely on the interior of the wheel.

"Some *diccobs*," bn Bem explained to his mesmerized audience, "only one or two new combinations can manage. Premier's *diccob* can do twenty nearly. Is prizewinner."

"I can imagine," McCoy said. "My stomach does flip-flops just watching it."

"Is the *diccob* the most flexible form of Pandronian life?" Spock inquired curiously, "or are there other native types equally adjustable?"

"Difficult to answer that question is," bn Bem began, his tone oddly thoughtful. "To understand, first you must know that on Pandro is—"

The commander's reply was interrupted by a soft chime. Everyone turned toward the direction of the sound.

One of the numerous doors on the other side of the room opened inward and two Pandronians entered the chamber. One appeared to be slightly younger than Commander bn Bem, while the other, judging from his movements and coloring, was of an advanced age. Touches of yellow had crept into his natural blue skin, and he walked toward them with the deliberate caution of the incipient infirm.

Commander bn Bem bowed before him as Kirk, Spock, and McCoy did their awkward best to imitate the gesture.

"I present the Supreme Integral of all Pandro," bn Bem announced grandiosely as he returned to an upright position, "Premier Kau afdel Kaun. This Other One I know not," he concluded in referring to the premier's companion.

"Greetings to you, bn Bem Commander. To you greetings also, Federation representatives, and thanks be for your returning the commander home," the premier said in a shaky voice. "For you back to be is good, Commander, though sorry This One is that your visit and study of Federation must interrupted so shockingly and suddenly be."

Despite his aged body, the premier spoke in English for the benefit of his alien guests, Kirk noted admiringly. There was no condescension in his voice, and neither was there the arrogance the captain had come to associate with Pandro: a result, Kirk decided, of the premier's long association with the missing Tam Paupa.

He began gesturing to the younger Pandronian at his

side. "Be known to Lud eb Riss, Commander and visitors. Of the atrocity on us visited he will tell you. This One tires." On unsteady legs the premier mounted the dais and slumped into the chair behind the curved desk.

"At the wall here," the younger Pandronian indicated, leading them to a blank space near the dais. Depressing a segmented tile caused a large map to descend. It was filled with Pandronian glyphs which none of the Federation officers could read, but a two-dimensional map was difficult to misinterpret no matter what its origin. Kirk felt certain he could identify large cities, mountains, an ocean, and other features.

"Was stolen the Tam Paupa," eb Riss told them, "several"—and he uttered a term in Pandronian which was evidently untranslatable—"ago. Thus far to it recover all efforts failed have."

With a hand he indicated a large symbol in the approximate center of the map. "We know it is not in Tendrazin or in any of other cities secondary nearby. Still scoured are other major cities of Pandro being. Search and seizing of known elements criminal nothing has produced. All are outraged by theft of Tam Paupa too."

"That's surprising," McCoy commented. "Why should the theft of the Tam Paupa bother them?"

"History has shown that crime flourishes best under stable governments, Doctor."

"Even on Vulcan?"

"Such sociological aberrations, Doctor, are more typical of less advanced societies such as—"

"Spock, Bones," Kirk muttered a warning. Both men returned their attention to eb Riss as if nothing had been said.

The Pandronian's hand moved to encircle a huge shaded area near Tendrazin, which grew to encompass a considerable section of the map west of the capital city.

"Has never been fully explored this region," eb Riss explained for their benefit. "Development halted here at Tendrazin. In this vast area we suspected the *ibillters*

who have defiled Pandro have the Tam Paupa taken."
eb Riss turned to stare at them, but his gaze was
concentrated principally on bn Bem.

"Is thought that none there can survive, yet investi-
gators believe perpetrators of blasphemy there have
fled. Explained can be, since *ibillters* probably insane
are."

"To the *varbox* fled?" an appalled bn Bem gasped.
"Mad are they for surely."

"Why surely?" Kirk wanted to know. "What is this
varbox?".

"A region filled with wild integrals and integrators,
so dense and swampish to enter there is to court death
in fashions unimaginable and certain."

"One thing I still don't understand," Kirk continued.
"How can your capital city be built so close to a dangerous, unexplored wilderness?"

"Much of Pandro unexplored is, Outworlder," eb
Riss snorted with typical Pandronian contempt. "You
comprehend not."

"We admit we know very little of Pandro," Spock
confessed. "We would like to know more. When formal
association between Pandro and the Federation takes
place, we—"

"*If* takes place," eb Riss snapped brusquely. "I explain simple for you. Are surrounded most of our cities
by largely untraveled jungle wildernesses. Is due to
nature of Pandronian biology. Is no such thing as Pandronian science of biology."

McCoy almost smiled. "Now, simple or not, that's
impossible."

"Listen clear, McCoy Doctor," bn Bem advised him.
"Are constantly changing, Pandronian lifeforms. Most
shapes unstable and ever altering, like *diccob* without
training. A few integrators like ourselves"—he indicated his own body and its three independent sections—"discovered long ago that to stay in permanent
association was benefit to all parts. Others have likewise evolved.

"But for rest of much of Pandro life, existence is
struggling continual to find satisfying combination of

sections. So is ever changing much of Pandro zoology, and some plant life as well. How can one classify species which exist a few days only?"

"I see," Spock murmured. "Pandro's ecology is unstable. I assume, Commander, that such steady mutations are limited to the higher forms of life?"

"They'd have to be, Spock," McCoy pointed out.

"Is true," bn Bem confirmed, "or otherwise ever altering diseases, bacteriums and virus forms, would all Pandro life have wiped out long ago. But forms microscopic constant are. Permanent integrators like self can build resistance to others."

"Is why," eb Riss put in, "all Pandronian cities and towns with history have old fortress walls around them, built by ancestors to hold out dangerously changing jungle lifes."

"What I still don't understand," muttered McCoy, "is why anyone would want to steal your Tam Paupa. If even the criminal elements have an investment in keeping it where it belongs, who does that leave as a potential thief?"

"Would only we know that ourselves, outworlder," came the sad voice of Premier afdel Kaun from behind the great desk. "Unheard of is this thing." He winced and both hands went to the sides of his head. "Is certain one thing only: Unless Tam Paupa soon recovered is, This One will lose ability to make sound objective decisions."

The supreme ruler of Pandro assumed a woeful expression. "Is certain. Can feel already This One divisiveness and personal opinions entering mind. At same time slips away slow and steady the intelligence needed to govern Pandro. Is terrible helpless this feeling."

"We must Tam Paupa recover, Kirk Captain," an anxious bn Bem added. "Or Pandro society sinks again into mindless raging against self." The commander drew himself up. "Have done what of you was asked, Kirk Captain, in bringing This One home. To you and your government goes thanks of planet Pandro."

Spock leaned over and whispered to Kirk, "Remember, Captain, our opportunity to gain a decisive march on the Klingons by ingratiating ourselves forever in the minds of the Pandronians."

"I haven't forgotten, Mr. Spock," the captain replied. He faced the raised desk and directed his words to the premier. "Perhaps a new approach, or the benefit of outside thought processes, would be of some help to you, sir."

"Yourselves explain," afdel Kaun implored.

"Well," Kirk continued, "from what we've learned so far, we know that Pandronian science is far advanced in certain fields. Yet the Federation is more advanced in others. We're not afraid of the *varbox*."

"Bravery of ignorance," snorted eb Riss, but Kirk ignored him and pressed on.

"We have certain weapons in our possession, unknown on Pandro, which would be of much help in making one's way through the jungle you fear so strongly."

"Is true," bn Bem confirmed.

"Enough intelligence I retain to know that to accept your offer of aid is wiseness," the premier said solemnly. "How soon can you join expedition into *varbox?*"

"Inside an hour," Kirk replied quickly. "We'd like to return to our ship briefly to outfit ourselves properly for the journey, and also to obtain heavier weaponry. We'll need something more than hand phasers if the inhabitants of this jungle are as intimidating as you make them sound."

"Danger lies in not knowing what one may confront, Kirk Captain," bn Bem told him. "Time we will save if you beam back down into *zintar* yards."

"Whatever you say, Commander," Kirk replied, not bothering to inquire as to what a *zintar* yard might be. They would know soon enough. He flipped open his communicator as Spock noted a new set of coordinates.

"Kirk to *Enterprise*."

"*Enterprise*—Scott here, Captain."

"Beam us up, Mr. Scott, and stand by the transporter. We'll be coming back down shortly."

"Aye, Captain." A pause, then, "Back down, Captain?"

"That's right, Scotty. It looks like we're going to see more of Pandro than we originally thought. . . ."

V

After drawing jungle fatigues, appropriate survival equipment, and type-two mounts for their hand phasers, the three officers beamed down to the surface of Pandro once again.

A *zintar* yard turned out to be an enormous stable, although Kirk was reminded more of a repair yard for large shuttlecraft. Rank on rank of the huge, barnlike metal sheds were arranged alongside one another before a broad sward of green growth, cut short like grass.

Each long metal cell contained a sinuous reptilian creature which was a near analog of the ancient, idealized Terran Chinese dragon. But these were covered with gray, brown, and green fur.

"Like my own people," bn Bem informed them, "has found the *zintar* a combination of integrals advantageous to maintain. Advantageous to us as well." The commander introduced them to a tall, swarthy-looking Pandronian who sported short whiskers and managed to look like the Pandronian equivalent of a pirate.

"This is ab Af, who will our *zintar* in charge of be." ab Af made a curt gesture indicative more of a being interested in minding his own business than of standard Pandronian arrogance.

"eb Riss and six others will arrive to join soon," bn Bem continued. "They a third *zintar* will ride, while will a second supplies carry. *Zintar* is only creature by us tamed which not afraid of forest. Better than machine. *Zintar* runs off other Pandronian life and will not break down. Very little there is that a *zintar* is afraid of."

"I can believe that," Kirk agreed, staring up at the weaving, bobbing dragon-head of the forty-meter-long creature. It yawned elaborately, displaying thin, needle-like teeth in front and flat grinders behind. Four spikes or stiff whiskers—Kirk couldn't decide which—dangled from the front corners of upper and lower jaws.

bn Bem directed them to step aside as ab Af urged the monster out of its stable. The handler utilized verbal commands and prods from a small charged metal tube.

Kirk noticed the wide saddles set between protruding vertebrae on the creature's back even as bn Bem asked, "If all are ready, Kirk Captain?"

McCoy ran a hand through his hair as he examined the attenuated apparition. "I don't know if all are," was his comment, "but as long as I'm not expected to feed one of these oversized horned toads, I guess I'll give it a try."

"Good is, McCoy Doctor," bn Bem complimented him. He barked something in Pandronian to ab Af. The handler stood to one side of the swaying skull, touched the *zintar* between the front legs, and shouted a command.

Docile as a dog, the six-legged colossus appeared to collapse in on itself. Its short, stumpy legs never moved, but the central body slumped to the ground between them, like a ship being lowered between six hydraulic lifts. Its stomach scraped the dirt.

"Intriguing arrangement of ligaments and muscles," was Spock's observation at this unexpected physiological maneuver. "Both appear to be extraordinarily flexible." Using the thick fur for handholds, the first officer mounted one of the Pandronian saddles notched into the animal's backbone and seated himself as best he could. Kirk and McCoy followed, the captain envying the ease with which eb Riss and his six armed followers mounted their *zintar* nearby.

Once everyone was properly seated—Kirk felt "aboard" would be a better term to describe mounting a creature this size—ab Af uttered another command. Kirk felt himself rising, a sensation not unlike that pro-

duced in one of the *Enterprise*'s turbolifts, as the *zintar*
raised its body between its legs again.

Then they were on their way, moving at a surpris-
ingly rapid pace through the wide streets of Tendrazin.
McCoy had started in surprise when the *zintar* began
to move. The movements beneath him were unique. It
was a peculiar—but not necessarily uncomfortable—
sensation, he reflected. Had he ever ridden a large
camel, the motion would have been somewhat more
familiar to him.

Before Kirk had gotten his fill of the fascinating architecture around them—a curious and exciting mixture of archaic and ultramodern—they had passed
through a very old, heavily guarded gate in the ancient
city wall and were traveling steadily across a broad
open plain.

"Many of our crops," bn Bem lectured them from
his position just behind ab Af, "are grown within old
city walls, to protect the cultivators from incursions by
wild Pandronian lifes. Space here and around most cities are clear kept for reason the same, Kirk Captain."

"We are obviously headed on some predetermined
course," Spock commented from two places behind
Kirk. "Why this way? I thought you said you didn't
have any idea where the thieves had fled, except into
the very large area you called the *varbox*."

"Are going that way now," bn Bem replied. "Have
tried all sources in cities. Was one noncity theory
which implicated *varbox,* but could not get Pandronians to try until you your weapons aid offered." His
voice turned conspiratorial.

"Several citizens of Tendrazin home returning from
fraternal meeting one night reported encountering large
group of nervous-seeming Pandronians leaving city by
gate now behind us. Suspicious Ones were on *coryats*
mounted. One citizen asked destination and Nervous
One replied his group to Cashua going. Cashua a
medium-sized city several hundred *laggets* to northeast
of Tendrazin."

"What's so suspicious about people going from one
city to another?" McCoy wanted to know.

"Not where—when," bn Bem told him. "No One travels at night near forests on Pandro if not in armored vehicles. Also, *coryats* good forest walkers, if protected well.

"Only recently this report checked in detail," the commander continued. "Was found that time necessary to travel between Tendrazin and Cashua, even allowing for reasonable delays, should have shown travelers there within four *daams*. No party on *coryats*, or of similar number to that reported by citizens, ever seen arriving at Cashua or other nearby cities. Party not sighted by aerial surveyests.

"So ground from Tendrazin outward hunted for clues. Many tracks of vehicles and animals near city, but few near forest. Found prints of *coryats* entering forest. Entering forest *there*," and he pointed ahead of them, to a slight break in the marching ranks of green and brown.

"Is old hunter trail, one of many," he went on. "No other trail show signs of *coryat* passage. May not be significant. Many Pandronians enter jungle on own, some for reasons legal not. Few return after long stay. Maybe these not wish to return.

"Is lucky dry season this is. If they did enter forest here, *coryat* tracks will remain."

In a short while the *zintars* slowed, approaching the first fringe of jungle. A small group of soldiers was waiting to greet them. eb Riss's *zintar* did the body-slumping trick and eb Riss dismounted to confer with one of the soldiers, apparently an officer. There was a short, animated discussion during which both Pandronians studied something on the ground out of Kirk's vision. He could imagine what the subject of their conversation was: the *coryat* tracks, which these troops had doubtlessly been placed here to protect against destruction—intentional or otherwise.

eb Riss confirmed Kirk's suspicions when he passed by them on the way back to his own *zintar*. "Tracks remain still," he called up to them. "Party of six to twelve entered the *varbox* here. Is more than first guessed. Too large surely it is for a larking group."

"True that is," agreed bn Bem, while Kirk and the others wondered at the purpose of a larking party. "On our way to hurry."

eb Riss gestured confirmation and trotted back to scramble monkeylike up the leg of his *zintar*. The expedition plunged into the forest.

Immediately the usefulness of the *zintar* in such terrain manifested itself. Not only did the creature's size intimidate and frighten off potential attackers, but its bulk shouldered aside or smashed over much vegetation, some of which was dense enough to impede the progress of any ground vehicle. The *Enterprise*'s heavy groundcraft could have done as well, but not nearly at such a pace.

Kirk mentioned his opinion as he continued to study the uneven, swampy ground below, which was thickly overgrown with alien roots and climbers. And this was supposed to be a trail!

"I can see why the Pandronians prefer organic to mechanical transportation, Spock."

"Indeed, Captain," the first officer agreed, eyeing a particularly wicked-looking cluster of thorny vines which the *zintar* simply strode through without apparent ill effects. "Even a powerful landcraft would sacrifice mobility for movement here. And there is also the matter of logistics. It is evident that the *zintars* can live well off the land."

They were many hours into the jungle when the head tracker shouted back to them from his position on eb Riss's mount. Handlers halted their *zintars* while the Pandronian scrambled down one postlike leg and examined the ground. He gestured and babbled until several other troopers dismounted and followed him into the dense underbrush to one side of the forest path. The greenery swallowed them up quickly.

bn Bem and eb Riss started to show signs of nervousness when the tracking party failed to call out or return some minutes later. The two officers were about to order the *zintars* into off-trail pursuit in search of their vanished comrades when the little group reappeared.

The head tracker looked disheveled and tired, but the excitement was evident in his face. He walked to stand below eb Riss, began talking rapidly and with many gestures.

"The tracker says," bn Bem translated for them as the discussion progressed, "that a small but definite animal path within lies. Is evidence also of *coryats* passing. Age of tracks," and now the commander was hard pressed to restrain his own enthusiasm, "is proper to correspond with time suspicious party was noted leaving Tendrazin. Is further confirmation to clinch in tracker's hand."

Kirk leaned as far to his right as he dared, squinting. The slim tracker was waving what looked from this distance to be a torn bit of black fabric. At bn Bem's request, the incriminating cloth was passed up to him. A brief inspection and then he was conferring with eb Riss in Pandronian while Kirk, Spock, and McCoy waited tensely for information.

eb Riss's *zintar* handler shouted and tapped his mount on its shoulder with the charged tube. One by one the three great creatures turned like seagoing ships to bull their way into the growths on their right. After a short walk the dense brush thinned somewhat, enough for Kirk and the others to see that they were truly traveling down a cleared and marked trail. It wasn't as broad or well used as the hunter's path they had entered the forest by, but a path it was.

bn Bem turned in his saddle, passed the bit of black material back to Kirk. His face looked grim. "Is first possible explanation to part of puzzlings, Kirk Captain. Now things become clear a little maybe."

"It's just a rag to me," Kirk told him, turning to pass it back to Spock. "Where's the significance for you?"

"A popular color on Pandro black is not, Captain. May again mean nothing. Is little to be gained by to conclusions hopping, but still . . ."

"But still—" Kirk prompted.

"Is on Pandro," the commander explained, "a small society of"—he paused for a second, hunting for a proper translation—"best I can come is physiological anarchists. They believe that holding integration to form perpetuating species is against natural orders. Would have all Pandro lifes, including This One, return to separate integrators and recombine as do wild forms. Mad Ones believe better integration than present developers of Pandronian civilization will eventually result.

"Very young and stupid most of them are. But they believe strongly in their madness, Kirk Captain. Have been troublesome in few incidents past, but not really dangerous. Is conceivable they could react violent enough against Pandronian heritages to perform heinous deed like theft of Tam Paupa. If any Pandronians could, would be them for sure.

"Part of their belief is to wear heavy black clothing, as if to hide the shame of their integration from universe."

"I take it the Tam Paupa was always well guarded," Spock said.

"Well guarded truly, Spock Commander," concurred bn Bem.

"I am puzzled, then," the first officer confessed, "as to how a small coterie of mildly annoying revolutionaries could suddenly jump from being youthfully irksome to executing a deed as elaborate as the Tam Paupa's theft."

"Agree wholesomely—no, wholeheartedly," bn Bem replied after a moment's consideration. "Is most strangeness. Would indeed not give group credit for such talents." He performed the Pandronian equivalent of a shrug.

"May be more than anarchist types after all. Into place pieces beginning to assemble. Still is missing important integers."

Kirk, Spock, and McCoy could only agree.

An urgent beep sounded in the Main Transporter Room on board the *Enterprise*. Transporter Chief Kyle stared blankly at it for a moment, then moved quickly to the console intercom when the beep was repeated.

"Transporter Room to bridge, Engineer Kyle speaking."

"Chief Scott here. What is it, Mr. Kyle?"

The engineer waited until a third beep confirmed the previous message and reported, "Sir, I'm receiving a direct nonverbal emergency signal from the surface on personal communicator frequency. There seems to be," and he hurriedly checked two readouts, "sufficient strength to indicate that the signal is being generated simultaneously by two—no, by three communicators."

A short pause, then, "It must be the captain, Mr. Spock, and Dr. McCoy, though I canna imagine why they're usin' nonverbal signalin'. They can tell us soon. Home in on them and stand by to beam 'em up, Mr. Kyle. We'll find out what happened soon enough."

On the bridge Scott turned to face Communications. "Lieutenant Uhura?"

"Mr. Scott?" the communications officer replied.

"See if you can raise any of the landin' party and get an explanation of what the trouble is."

"Yes, sir." Uhura turned back to her instruments and rapidly manipulated controls. She glanced back concernedly seconds later.

"No response, sir."

"Verra well." He directed his words to the command chair pickup again. "Beam 'em up quickly, Mr. Kyle."

"Aye, aye, Mr. Scott."

"Rematerialize slow as you safely can. I'm coming down." He rose from the chair. "Lieutenant Uhura, you're in command until I return with the captain."

"Very well, sir." As a precaution, she buzzed for Lieutenant M'ress to come on duty, on the unlikely chance that she would have to vacate Communications and take up position at the command station. Safety procedures were good to keep up, even if certain key personnel lost a little sleep in the process.

Moving at maximum speed, Scott entered the Transporter Room even as Kyle was bringing up the crucial levers.

"They're coming in now, Chief," the engineer indicated, sparing the approaching officer the briefest of glances.

"Carry on, Mr. Kyle."

Three forms slowly solidified, began to assume definite outlines in the transporter alcove. The last flickers of transporter energy were dying away as Scott charged reflexly for the alarm switch.

The paralysis beam projected by one of the forms standing in the alcove caught the chief engineer just above the knees. With a desperate twist and lunge, Scott was just able to fall forward far enough to slap a hand down on the red control.

Klaxons commenced sounding all over the *Enterprise*. On the bridge, Uhura declared a general alert, then activated the command chair intercom.

"Transporter Room—Chief Scott, Mr. Kyle, what's happening down there?"

Kyle fought to reply even as he was dodging immobilizing beams from behind the shielding bulk of the console. Scott fought to pull himself out of the line of fire using only his hands.

"I don't know!" the transporter engineer shouted toward the intercom pickup. "Chief Scott's been hurt." The three things in the alcove were rushing toward him, firing as they came. "Three boarders, bipedal, type un—"

Transmission from the Transporter Room ceased abruptly.

"Engineer Kyle—report," Uhura yelled into the intercom. "Report!" The intercom gave back a steady slight hiss—and faint sounds as of something not human moving about the chamber. She turned, spoke decisively to where a now wide-awake M'ress sat ready at the controls.

"Lieutenant, contact all security stations. Seal off the entire deck around the Main Transporter Room and have security personnel close in."

"Yes, sirr," M'ress acknowledged without thinking. "What arre they to look forr?"

"Three invaders, bipedal in form. Beyond that, your guess is as good as mine. Whatever they are, they've

injured both Chief Scott and Mr. Kyle. Warn Nurse
Chapel to stand by for casualties and to alert backup
medical personnel."

Uhura turned to face the helm as M'ress relayed her
orders through the ship. "Mr. Arex, maintain orbit and
begin attempts to contact the landing party. Mr. Sulu?"

"Yes, Lieutenant?"

"Take over security operations. You will personally
assume charge of the rescue of Chief Scott and Mr.
Kyle."

Sulu was out of his chair and heading for the turbolift. Uhura watched him leave, wishing she could go in
his place. But she had been left in command, and personal reasons were no reasons for altering orders—especially in an emergency situation. But, she thought
furiously, if the three who had beamed up weren't the
captain, Mr. Spock, and Dr. McCoy, then who were
they? More important, why weren't the *Enterprise* crew
members responding from Pandro?

In the Transporter Room below, Scott rolled over
onto his back and pushed himself to a sitting position
against a wall. Kyle, he saw, had been completely paralyzed by the strange weapon which had so far only affected the chief engineer from the waist down. Around
him the general alert continued to sound, but it didn't
appear to panic or otherwise affect the three figures
standing over Kyle and conferring among themselves.

Each was clad in a long black robe. Black hoods
covered their heads. At the same time as Scott recognized their chatter as Pandronian they flipped their
hoods back and began to disrobe. They were Pandronians, all right.

Somewhat to the chief's surprise, Commander Ari
bn Bem wasn't in the group. He was glad of that. Had
bn Bem been one of the belligerent boarders, it would
have meant that the captain and the others were in
serious trouble below. They still might be, but the
wild-eyed, disorganized appearance of these three gave
Scott some hope that at least the Pandronian government wasn't involved.

But if that was the case, how had these creatures managed to board the *Enterprise* so neatly?

All were sullen and grim-faced. One pointed at Scott, then jabbered at his companions. A second replied curtly and they bent to examine Engineer Kyle.

Scott ground his teeth in frustration and anger as they roughly turned the body over. With relief Scott saw that Kyle's eyes were open and functioning, even if the rest of his body was frozen into immobility.

Further discussion in the alien tongue and suddenly the three Pandronians became nine. Each split into its three component parts while Scott gaped. He knew of the Pandronian ability from the report of what had transpired on Delta Theta Three, but this was the first time he had actually seen the process in action—not to mention in triplicate.

Each section grasped a sidearm in various hands, toes, or cilia, and the three heads, three torsos, and three lower bodies ambled out the Transporter Room door. As it shut behind them, Scott moved, fighting to drag himself toward the intercom.

He had no idea what the Pandronians were up to other than that it was inimical to the good health of the ship and its crew. And, he realized with a start, he had reported three of them. Without knowing that the invaders were Pandronians, Uhura and everyone else would be hunting for only three shapes, leaving six sections to stroll freely about the ship.

Hopefully they would be detected as sections of mature Pandronians, but Scott had no intention of leaving that identification to others. Despite the fact that the paralysis seemed to grow worse the more he moved, he continued hunching and pulling himself across the deck. The tingling numbness had reached his waist by the time he reached the console.

Exhausted by the effort, he started to shout. The intercom should still be open, since the Pandronians hadn't bothered to shut it off. If so, the directional pickup should gather and transmit his voice.

But the tingling moved rapidly now, creeping eerily up his arms and chest and into his throat. He couldn't operate his voice. Screaming furiously with his eyes, he slumped to the deck, falling across the legs of the motionless transporter engineer and rolling slightly to one side.

Apparently the paralysis left the higher functions unimpaired, for Scott found he could still see and hear, could still think clearly. Moving his eyes, he saw Kyle staring helplessly back at him. With silent glances the two men managed to communicate a wealth of emotions to each other. Not least was a mutual anger at their inability to warn the rest of the ship as to the nature of their attackers.

A patrol of three security personnel was first to spot the invaders. Phasers set on stun, they exchanged fire with the unrecognized antagonists. Incredibly agile and too small to hit easily, the aliens slipped away.

But now the crew knew what they were up against, for the ensign in charge had recognized the similarity of the sectioned creatures to a former passenger.

"Pandronians!" Uhura exclaimed. "I don't understand." She leaned a little closer to the pickup to make certain she heard correctly. "Was Commander Ari bn Bem, our former visitor, among those firing back at you?"

"It's impossible to say, Lieutenant," came the reply from the security officer. "But from the pictures we were shown of him and from the couple of times I myself met him in corridors, I don't think so. Of course, there's no way to tell, and they were all split up in parts. Nine parts. I guess they could even be in disguise."

"Thank you, Ensign," Uhura acknowledged. "Keep your phasers set on stun. They haven't killed anyone yet. If they do," she added warningly, "appropriate orders will be forthcoming."

She clicked off, turned to Communications. "Lieutenant M'ress, keep trying to contact the landing party."

"I'm doing so, Lieutenant Uhurra, but therre seems to be some kind of interrferrence."

"Natural or artificial?" Uhura demanded to know.

"I don't know yet, Lieutenant. Without detailed in-forrmation on Pandrro, it is difficult to say." She turned back to her instruments, leaving Uhura frustrated and unsatisfied, but helpless to do more than wait.

The squad that had originally spotted the invaders turned down a corridor. Three dim shapes could be seen scuttling around a far bend.

"There they are!" the ensign in charge yelled. "Come on!"

Phasers at the ready, the two men and one woman rushed down the corridor. Each got halfway to the turn the three shapes had vanished behind when they grabbed at midsection or head, tumbling one after another to the deck.

Three sets of arms and chests slipped out of a crevice to inspect the motionless shapes lying on the metal flooring. Two lower torsos with heads set incongruously in their middles came around the corridor bend they had previously turned. The heads jumped off the hips, made room for the middle torsos and arms, which then picked the heads up and set them on their respective shoulders.

Thus reassembled, the three Pandronians started back up the corridor the way the security team had come.

VI

The *zintars* continued to make rapid progress through the forest. Kirk, Spock, and McCoy used the deceptively tranquil ride to marvel at the incredible diversity of life around them. Such abundance of forms was only natural in a world of constantly changing species, where an entire genus might consist of only one creature. And that creature might choose to annihilate itself and its place in any textbook of Pandronian biology by freely dissolving into its multiple components, or integrals.

These endlessly variable animals were in never-ceasing competition to create a form more successful, better able to compete, than the next. The steady flux led to a number of forms bizarre beyond belief, forms which—bn Bem told them—rarely lasted out a day or more before the component integrals realized their own absurdity.

They saw tiny mouse-sized creatures with enormous heads and pincushion mouths full of teeth, impressive but impractical on creatures so small. Massive armored bodies teetered precariously on the lithe limbs of running herbivores. Tall bipedal trunks armed with clawed arms and legs ended in bovine faces filled with flat molars suitable for mashing only the softest of vegetable matter.

"Such extreme mismatches ludicrous are, Kirk Captain," the commander pointed out. "Outlandish shapes continue to join, though, brief as they may last. So fierce is the compulsion new forms to create."

"How many possible combinations are there?" asked a thoroughly engrossed McCoy. "How many varieties of hands and legs, torsos and heads, trunks and so on exist?"

bn Bem looked dolefully back at him. "No one knows, McCoy Doctor. Have been already cataloged many hundreds of thousands of shapes and millions of integrals. Sometimes cataloged ones vanish and new ones take their place. Is impossible job which never ends."

"I see," an impressed McCoy replied. "How often does a new successful form, like yourself or the *diccob* or *zintar* evolve?"

"Cannot give figure," bn Bem responded, "but is rare occurence. About forty percent Pandronian lifes maintain permanent association and reproduce same form. All can break down, though, if such is natural willing, but this is very rare. Cannot tell what will find next."

The officers were soon to discover the truth of the

commander's concluding statement. The group made camp in a partial clearing on a slight rise of ground. Gentle though the rise was, it placed them high enough above the surrounding terrain to provide reasonably dry footing.

Kirk studied their surroundings. Only the different colors and designs of the encircling vegetation, the peculiar alien cries filling the evening air, made this jungle any different from half a hundred others he had visited or read about, including those of Earth itself.

To the south, the Pandronian sun was slowly sinking. It was slightly larger and redder than Sol, a touch hotter as well. The three massive *zintars* were bedded away from the camp, where they made their own clearing by simply walking in tighter and tighter circles until trampled vegetation formed a soft bed underneath. Well trained, they were left by themselves, their handlers secure in the knowledge that nothing known would risk attacking them.

eb Riss and his men unpacked supplies from the third pseudodragon, taking care not to tangle lines in the creature's fur. They produced several oddly shaped, roughly globular tents and some equally odd foot stores, which bn Bem assured Spock he and the others could eat. Had he not partaken with reasonable satisfaction of food on board the *Enterprise*?

The bonfire the troops raised in the middle of the encampment was the only familiar thing around, and McCoy in particular was glad for its cheery crackle and sputter.

"You can always count on the familiarity of a fire," he pointed out to his companions, "no matter what kind of world you're on."

"That is not necessarily true, Doctor," Spock mused. "Depending both on the nature of the atmosphere in question and the combustible materials employed, a fire could be—"

"Never mind," McCoy advised with a sigh. "Sorry I mentioned it, Spock."

A heavy mist closed in around them as the sun dropped lower in the sky. The nature of the yelps and squeeps from the surrounding jungle changed slightly as the creatures of the day faded into their holes and boles and the inhabitants of dark gradually awoke.

"I can see," Kirk found himself musing conversationally to bn Bem, "how Pandronians could develop a feeling of superiority to other races."

"A conceit to be deplored,'" the reformed commander responded.

"No, it's true," Kirk insisted. "You're not to be blamed, I think, for such an attitude. You live on a world of constant change. Coping with such change is an incredible racial feat. You have reason to have developed considerable pride."

"Is so," bn Bem was unable to refrain from concurring.

Their conversation was shattered by a violent yet muffled howl from the depths of the forest.

"What was that?" McCoy blurted.

"Is no telling, McCoy Doctor," bn Bem reminded him, eyeing the surrounding trees appraisingly. "Is as your saying, as good as mine is your guess."

"Generally," Spock ventured, striving to see through the opaque wall of emerald, "those creatures which make the loudest noises do so because they have no fear of calling attention to themselves. That roar was particularly uninhibited."

As if to back up Spock's evaluation, the howl sounded again, louder, closer.

"I believe," the first officer said slowly, "it would be advisable to concoct some kind of defense. Whatever is producing that roar seems to be moving toward us."

"Is not necessarily true," bn Bem argued. "Strange vocal organs of Pandronian lifes can—"

Something not quite the size of a shuttlecraft rose like a purple moon in the almost dark, towering out of the underbrush. It bellowed thunderously, took a step toward the camp—and stopped. It had encountered a pair of huge trees too close together for it to pass between. It hammered with massive limbs at the trees, shrieking its outrage.

Fortunately, Kirk thought as he retreated toward the

bonfire in the center of the camp, the components which had combined to compose this creature had not included more than the absolute minimum of brains.

The creature snarled and howled at the tiny running shapes so close before it while continuing to try to force its way between the two trees. It could have backed off, taken several ponderous steps to either side on its five pairs of scaly legs, and charged the camp unimpeded. Thankfully, it obstinately continued battering at the stolid trees.

Kirk watched as the Pandronians struggled to set up a large complex device. It consisted of several shiny, featureless metal boxes arranged in seemingly random order. A long, rather childish-looking muzzle projected from one end of the collage and various controls from the other.

By now the thought had penetrated the attacking abomination's peanut mind that to go around might be more efficient than trying to go through. Backing up like a lumbering earth mover going into reverse, the creature moved to one side of the right-hand tree and started forward again.

Only its slowness allowed Kirk and his companions a measure of confidence. Kirk felt he could easily outrun the thing, but would prefer not to have to try. Spock was regarding the still-frantic Pandronians, and he concluded aloud, "It seems our friends were not expecting an assault of this size. I suggest, Captain, that to preserve the camp and supplies we disregard the egos of our hosts and restrain it ourselves."

McCoy already had his phaser out and was holding it aimed on the unbelievably slow carnivore. It showed a mouth lined with short saw-edged teeth. The cavity was wide and deep enough for a man to walk around in without stooping. Four eyes set in a neat row near the crest of the skull peered down at them dumbly, crimson in the glow of the campfire.

Nonetheless, McCoy wasn't impressed. "How can any meat-eater that slow expect to catch any prey? It's got to be an unstable form."

"True, Bones," Kirk acknowledged, "but if we don't stop it, it's going to make a mess of the camp."

"Maybe if we rubbed its tummy it would calm down a little," the doctor suggested.

Spock looked uncertain at the suggestion. "An interesting notion, Doctor. How do you propose we convince the creature to turn onto its back?"

"Don't look at me, Spock," McCoy responded innocently. "I just make up the prescription. I don't make the patient take it."

"I think something more convincing is in order, Bones," Kirk decided as the creature neared the first of the tents. "On command, fire."

Three beams brightened a small portion of the night. They struck the creature, one hitting the side of the skull near the neck, the other two touching higher up near the waving dorsal spines.

Letting out a hideous yowl, the monster halted. Two front feet rose off the ground, and the nightmare head jerked convulsively to one side. The creature shook off the effects, took another half tread forward.

"Again, *fire!*" Kirk ordered.

Once more the phaser beams struck; once again the effects were only temporary.

"Aim for the head," Kirk ordered, frowning at their inability to injure or even to turn the monster.

"Captain, we don't even know if that's where its integral brain is located," declared Spock, who shouted to make himself heard above the creature's snuffling and yowling.

"Why don't you ask it?" McCoy suggested as he tried to focus on one of the four pupils high above.

Spock frowned. "The creature does not appear capable of communication at the higher levels, Doctor." He fired and ducked backward as the head, making a sound like two steel plates crashing together, snapped in his direction.

But by now the Pandronians had assembled themselves behind their funny-looking little wheeled device. All at once there was a soft thud from the muzzle and something erupted from its circular tip.

Several hundred tiny needles struck the creature, distributed across its body. The creature took another step forward, the head almost within range of a quickly retreating Kirk, and then it stopped. All four eyes blinked sequentially; a second time. A high mewling sound began to issue from the beast, incongruously pitiful in so threatening a shape.

Then it started coming apart like a child's toy. Various segments—legs, tail parts, and pieces of skull—dropped off, each running madly in different directions, until the entire apparition had scattered itself into the jungle.

"That's quite a device," McCoy commented, impressed. He walked over to study the machine. It no longer looked funny. "What does it do?"

"Is difficult, McCoy Doctor," the Pandronian commander explained, "to kill a creature whose individual integrals retain life independent. Would have to kill each integral separately.

"This," and he indicated the weapon, "fires tiny syringes, each of which a chemical contains which makes mutual association abhorrent to creature's integrals. Is very effective." He gestured at the forest wall.

"Attacking carnivore integration suddenly found its components incompatible with one another. All broke free and fled themselves. Will not for a long time recombine because of lasting effects of the drug."

"I offer apologies," a new voice said. Kirk turned, saw a distraught eb Riss approaching them. "We did not an assault by so large a meat-eater expect, Kirk Captain. Was oversight in camp preparations on my part. Sorrowful I am."

"Forget it," advised Kirk.

"To produce a carnivore so large," eb Riss continued, "requires an unusually large number of integrators. The *fasir,*" and he indicated the device that had fired the hypodermic darts, "is not ordinarily prepared so large a dose to deliver. And the first time we certain had to be dose was large enough to disassemble creature, or half of it might have continued attack we could not stop in time."

"An interesting method of fighting an unusual and unpredictable opponent," observed Spock with appreciation. "It would be interesting to consider if such a drug could be effectively employed against non-Pandronian life forms. The fighting ability of another person, for example, would be severely impaired if his arms and legs could be induced to run in different directions. And if the parts could later be made to recombine, then a battle might be won without any permanent harm being done. There remains the question of psychological harm, however. If one were to literally lose one's head, for example . . ."

Mercifully, Kirk thought, McCoy said nothing.

"Is strange, though," bn Bem commented as he studied the forest, "to find so large a carnivore here. Far though we be, is still close for one so large to Tendrazin."

McCoy gestured at the jungle. "Do you think maybe it has a mate out there?"

Both bn Bem and eb Riss favored the doctor with a confused expression. "A mate? Ah!" bn Bem exclaimed, showing understanding. "Is evident you have no knowledge of Pandronian reproduction methods. Can become very complicated with multiple integrated beings. When we have year or two together will This One be pleased to explain Pandronian reproductive systems."

"Thanks," McCoy responded drily. "We'll pass on it for now."

"Any word on the whereabouts of the Pandronian boarders, Lieutenant?" Uhura inquired of M'ress.

"Nothing," came the prompt reply. Abruptly the communications officer placed a hand over the receiver in one fuzz-fringed ear. "Just a moment. Casualty rreport coming in."

Uhura's fingers tightened on the arms of the command chair.

"One securrity patrrol incapacitated—thrree total."

"How bad?" came the unwanted but unavoidable next question.

"They appearr to be subject to some forrm of muscularr parralysis. It is selective in that it does not affect the involuntarry musculaturre, perrmitting vital functions to continue." Something on the board above the console beeped for attention, and M'ress rushed to acknowledge.

"Anotherr rreporrt, frrom Sick Bay this time. Trransporrterr Chief Kyle and Lieutenant Commanderr Scott have been similarrly affected. Commanderr Scott has been only parrtially affected, it appearrs. He is waiting to talk to you now."

"Put him through," she snapped. "Mr. Scott?"

"I'm okay, Lieutenant Uhura."

"We know its Pandronians. What happened?"

"They came through as I was enterin' the Transporter Room. Surprise was total. They used some kind of hand weapon that puts your whole body to sleep—everything but your insides. I dinna know what they're up to, but there is one thing I do want to know—verra badly, lass."

"I'm thinking the same thing, Mr. Scott." She could almost hear him nod his agreement.

"Aye ... How did they know what frequency to simulate to convince us it was the captain and the others who wanted to be beamed back aboard?" There was a pause, then the chief engineer continued in a more speculative tone.

"The only thing I can think of is that they've taken the captain, Mr. Spock, and Dr. McCoy prisoner and learned or knew in advance how to broadcast the emergency signal."

A lighter but no less serious voice sounded over the communicator. "Now, you just lie down, Mr. Scott, and no more *but*'s, *if*'s, or *maybe*'s about it."

"Who's that?" Uhura inquired.

"Nurse Chapel here, Lieutenant," came the reply. "The paralysis shows no signs of worsening or spreading in any way which would threaten life functions. But I've four and a half cases in here, counting Mr. Scott as partly recovered. None of the others show any indication of similar recovery yet. I don't want to put any strain on anyone's system." She added, obviously for Scott's benefit. "No matter how well they're feeling."

"I agree absolutely," Uhura declared. "Let me know when anyone's condition changes—for better or worse."

"Will do, Lieutenant."

"Bridge out." Uhura turned back to stare thoughtfully at the communications station. Her gaze did not fall on the busy M'ress, who was striving to coordinate the flow of security reports from around the ship, but went past her.

How *had* the Pandronians known what signal to duplicate? And how had they managed to do it? Was Scott right? Had the captain and the others been captured? Or was there another, as yet unforseeable explanation?

An excited yelp came from Communications, a cross between a growl and a shout.

"Take it easy, Lieutenant M'ress," Uhura advised. "What is it?"

"I have contact with the landing parrty, Lieutenant!" she replied gleefully. "It's weak, but coming thrrough."

Uhura was hard pressed to keep her own enthusiasm in check. "Put them through."

There was a beep, followed by a burst of white noise. Exotic sounds drifted over the bridge speakers, but Uhura didn't relax even when she heard a familiar, if distorted and slightly puzzled, voice.

"Kirk here," the badly garbled acknowledgment came. "What's the trouble, Mr. Scott?"

"Mr. Scott has been injured, Captain," she said quickly. "This is Lieutenant Uhura, acting in command."

"Scotty hurt?" came the cry of disbelief. "What's going on up there, Lieutenant? Report in full."

"We've been boarded, Captain. By Pandronians— three of them." She hesitated, then asked, "Are you sure you're speaking freely? If you can't, try to give me some sort of sign."

There was a long pause and everyone on the bridge

could hear Kirk discussing the incredible situation with someone else. A new voice sounded.

"Spock here. We are perfectly all right, Lieutenant, and able to converse as freely as if we were at our stations. What is this about the ship's being boarded by Pandronians? Such a thing should not be possible. The Pandronians don't possess the requisite technology."

"I'm sorry, Mr. Spock, but I want to make sure you're okay. What are you doing now, and where are you?"

Mildly incredulous, the ship's first officer replied with forced calm, "We are at present aiding local authorities in an attempt to recover something called a Tam Paupa, which is vital to the maintenance of stable, friendly government on Pandro. That is not important at this time.

"What is important, Lieutenant, is how Pandronians, and hostile ones at that, succeeded in gaining access to the *Enterprise*."

"We don't know for certain," Uhura tried to tell them. "Somehow they managed to simulate the precise frequency of your hand communicators, in addition to duplicating the emergency beam-aboard signal in triplicate. Mr. Scott and Mr. Kyle naturally assumed *you* were broadcasting those signals and so locked in on them and beamed the villains aboard.

"Instead of you, three Pandronians appeared. They used some kind of paralysis weapon to stun the chief, Mr. Kyle, and at least one entire security patrol. Nurse Chapel says it doesn't appear to be fatal, but all five people affected are still immobile. Mr. Scott can talk, but that seems to be about all."

"What steps have you taken, Lieutenant?" Kirk demanded to know.

"All security forces have been mobilized and are now hunting the Pandronians, Captain," she reported. "The ship is on full alert, and all personnel are aware of the Pandronians' presence."

"What do they hope to achieve?" Kirk wondered aloud, static badly crippling the transmission.

"Excuse me, Captain," Spock broke in, "but it

seems clear that the Pandronians who boarded the *Enterprise* are in some way connected with those responsible for the theft of the Tam Paupa. Yet I do not understand how they could know we are aiding the government—or how they are performing technical feats supposedly beyond their capacity."

"I want answers, Mr. Spock, not more questions. Stand by, Uhura."

"Standing by, sir," she replied. There followed a period of intense discussion on the surface below, none of which came over the speakers understandably.

Arex used the interruption to address the command chair. "Lieutenant Uhura?"

"What is it, Mr. Arex?"

The navigator looked thoroughly confused. "It is only that in routine observation of the surface below us, I have recently detected something which may be of interest."

"What is it?"

The Edoan manipulated instrumentation. A topographic photomap of a large section of Pandro was projected by the main viewscreen forward. A cross-hair sight appeared, was adjusted to line up on the map's northeast quadrant. Several concentric circles of lightly shaded blue were superimposed over the region, the colors intensifying near the cross hairs.

"There seems to be an unexpectedly high level of controlled radiation active in this region," the navigator explained. "It is far more intense and sophisticated than anything else operating on Pandro, more concentrated even than anything in the capital city itself. It may be that it is a secret Pandronian installation."

"Just a second, Lieutenant Arex. M'ress, switch the lieutenant's intercom into the ship-to-ground broadcast." The Caitian communications officer executed the command, and Arex repeated the information for the benefit of those on the ground.

"Most interesting, Mr. Arex," came Spock's reply after the navigator had finished relaying his discovery. "Could you compare the center of radiant generation with our present position? Dr. McCoy will also activate his communicator to provide you with our most powerful detectable signal."

Several anxious moments followed during which M'ress pinpointed the source of the communicator broadcast. She then relayed the coordinates to Arex, who compared them with the location of the cross hairs on the photomap, then gave the information to Spock.

"*Most* interesting," the first officer replied in response, without bothering to indicate why it was so intriguing. "Thank you, Lieutenant."

"Uhura?" Kirk's voice sounded again. "Maintain red alert until the Pandronians are taken—alive, if possible. We believe they may have something to do with a tiny but dangerous rebel faction that opposes the constituted Pandronian government. But we don't know how they're doing what they're doing, or why.

"You can regard them as dangerous fanatics liable to try anything, no matter how insane. If they belong to the same group, they've already committed the ultimate act of outrage against their people. Consider humans in a similar position and treat these boarders likewise. But no killing if it can be avoided."

"We'll watch ourselves, Captain," Uhura assured him firmly. "Make sure you watch yourselves."

"Advice received and noted, Lieutenant. Contact us when something has been resolved—if you're able. The radiation Mr. Arex detected is undoubtedly responsible for our difficulties in communication. Kirk out."

"*Enterprise* out," Uhura countered.

Kirk put his communicator away, turned his attention to his first officer. Spock was making sketches on a small pad. "Tendrazin is here, Captain," he explained, indicating a small circle. "Our present position is approximately here, according to Mr. Arex's information."

Kirk called Commander bn Bem over and showed him Spock's sketch, explaining what the symbols meant.

"Yes, correct is," the Pandronian agreed, indicating

the distances and relationships of Tendrazin and their current location.

"We are traveling in this line," Spock continued, using stylus and pad to elaborate. "The source of the unusual radiation, as detected by instruments on our ship, Commander, lies about here." He tapped an *X* mark slightly north and west of their present position. "Almost in a direct line with our present course away from Tendrazin. Does the Pandronian government or any private Pandronian concern operate an installation in that area which might produce such radiants?"

"In the *varbox?*" bn Bem stammered unbelievingly. "I have from home away been, but not so long as that. But to make certain is always good idea." He called out in Pandronian.

eb Riss joined them, giving Spock's crude map sketch a quick, curious glance. "Have in this region," and bn Bem pointed to the radiation source, explaining its meaning, "any government posts been emplaced since my leaving?"

eb Riss's reaction was no less incredulous than the commander's. If anything, Kirk felt, it was more intense. "In that area lies nothing—nothing," he told them assuredly. "Is most intense and unwholesomest swampland. In such territories exist the most dangerous lifeforms in constant state of battle and recombination. No sane Pandronian would there go, and total Mad One would live not to reach it."

"Our readings wouldn't be off so drastically," Kirk informed him. "There is unquestionably a great deal of activity of a sophisticated nature going on there."

"Natural sources, maybe?" ventured eb Riss.

Kirk shook his head slowly. "Absolutely not. The quality and kind of radiation stamp it as artificial in source. If it was natural, Lieutenant Arex wouldn't have bothered to mention it to us unless it was dangerous."

"Is all very hard to believe," eb Riss muttered. "Certain is This One no representative of Pandro government there has been. No private group could build installation there, not even stealers of Tam Paupa. Must be mistaken your ship's detectors."

"Unlikely," Spock said sharply. "Nor is Lieutenant Arex the type to make such a report without triple-checking his readings."

"Are you so sure the rebels couldn't have a hideout in that area?" McCoy pressed bn Bem.

"Are mad and evil the blasphemers, McCoy Doctor," the commander admitted, "but suicidal are not. Remember, ourselves would not be here now if not with aid of your advanced energy weapons. Life forms here and certainly there would overwhelm These Ones, even with *fasir* to defend us. Mad Ones have no such helping." He looked to eb Riss for confirmation.

"To knowledge of This One, *no* Pandronian has ever entered great swamps—or at least, entered and come out again to tell of it." eb Riss indicated agreement.

"And still," Kirk murmured thoughtfully, "Arex insists there's something in there. Something throwing off a lot of controlled energy. Something that's been interfering with our communications to the *Enterprise*." He eyed bn Bem firmly.

"Whatever it is, it's not very far off our present path. It'll be interesting to see if your tracker leads us toward that area. Don't you think that would be a mite suspicious, if these *coryat* tracks curve toward the radiation source?"

"All may come to be, Kirk Captain," eb Riss admitted, "but if does, tracks will there end. Not best tracker on Pandro can follow prints in swamplands."

"They won't have to," Spock explained to the pessimistic Pandronian. He flourished the map sketch. "The *Enterprise* has located the source of radiation. If we turn toward it, we need only continue on through the swamp in its direction. If required, we can recheck our position at any time by contacting the ship. Provided," he added cautioningly, "communications interference grows no worse."

"Very well so," eb Riss said, dropping his objections. "If holds true, we must proceed toward *suspected* radiation source." Evidently the Pandronian officer still refused to believe that any Pandronians could have constructed something in the inimical swamplands. "But only if *coryat* tracks lead there and no place else."

"I disagree," bn Bem said firmly. Kirk and the others looked at the commander in surprise. "I enough have seen of Federation science facilities to know that what *Enterprise* officers say is truth." He gestured with a furry arm into the jungle ahead.

"Could be circling track designed to throw off any pursuings. Could follow we *coryat* tracks for many *fluvets* and find nothing save more *coryat* tracks. *Enterprise* findings to me significant are. I think we to radiation source should proceed, no matter where go *coryat* prints."

"I concur not, Commander," objected eb Riss strongly. When bn Bem merely stared back, the other Pandronian made a hand movement indicative of resignation. "But is outranked This One. It as you say will be."

"*Slateen*," bn Bem announced in Pandronian. "Is settled, then. We toward there turn," and he pointed to the *X* on Spock's map.

eb Riss headed back to ready his own troops and to mount the lead *zintar*. As McCoy walked toward his own patiently waiting dragon he jerked a thumb toward the forest, toward the two huge trees their assailant of the previous night had tried to break through.

"Apparently," he told bn Bem, "we're heading into an especially bad area. Does that mean we're likely to encounter any more visitors like last night's?"

"Is not likely, McCoy Doctor," the commander informed him.

McCoy was surprised, but relieved. bn Bem added, "Creature that attacked us last night would not be able to compete with dangerous animals in swamplands."

"Oh," was all McCoy said, trying to conjure up an image of something that could take the monster of the forest apart integral by integral.

"Surely the thought of confronting larger primitive

carnivores does not intimidate you, Doctor," Spock declared. "You have faced far more dangerous creatures on other worlds, which could not stand up to a type-two phaser."

"It's not that, Spock," the doctor explained. "It's just that the Pandronians don't even know what might be festering and growing out there. How can they, when potential antagonists break up and form new combinations every couple of days? I can take the thought of coming up against all kinds of different killers, but the idea of facing something never before in existence until it stands up and screams in your ear, and doing that maybe a couple of times a day, is a bit overpowering."

"It does reduce one's ability to prepare for defense," the first officer had to admit. "Still, that only adds to the interest of the occasion. Imagine being able to remain in one place for a while and watch evolution take place around you."

"Thanks just the same, Spock," McCoy replied. "Me, I think I'd prefer a little more biological stability." And he shivered slightly in a cool morning breeze as the howls, hoots, and shrieks of creatures which had only just come into being sounded the arrival of a new day.

VII

The low-intensity blast of a phaser set on stun exploded on the wall behind one of the three Pandronians. That was followed immediately by a distant cry of "There they are! Notify all other units."

The Pandronian that the bolt had just missed shouted to his companions. Together they increased their pace as they ran down the corridor.

In addition to hearing the faint call with their own auditory organs, the boarders had also detected it far more clearly over the pocket communicators each of them carried. Although those communicators differed substantially from Federation issue, they still received the on-board broadcasts of the *Enterprise* with shocking electronic competence.

Their very presence was something no one—not Scott, not Uhura, nor anyone else striving to locate the three intruders—could have suspected. So even as instructions to various security units and the rest of the crew were being sent through the ship, the Pandronians who were the subject of all the conversation were overhearing every word.

At that very moment the interlopers were listening to instructions passed to a large security team close ahead, directing them to block off the corridor. While the three had managed to evade the group which had nearly caught up with them, they knew that couldn't last much longer. More and more security teams were concentrating in this area, sealing off every possible escape route.

Or so they thought.

Realizing the importance of the narrowing cluster of pursuers, the Pandronians did a curious thing. They stopped. The tallest of the three fumbled with his backpack and removed a small box. A tiny screen was set on top of it with controls below.

Once activated, the screen began to display a rapidly shifting series of schematics and diagrams. Not everyone could have recognized them, but an engineer would have known what they were instantly. They displayed, in excellent detail, the inner construction of a Federation heavy cruiser.

The operator touched a switch, freezing one diagram on the screen. All three Pandronians examined it. This was followed by a brief, intense discussion after which they hurried on down the corridor once more.

Very soon they came to a small subcorridor. Instead of rushing past, they turned down it. The subcorridor was a dead end, according to the diagram, but the Pandronians were not looking for an appropriate place to be captured or commit suicide.

Stopping near the end of the subcorridor, one of

them opened a carefully marked door on the right. It opened into a cramped room, two walls of which were lined with controls. The largely automatic devices were not what interested the Pandronians, however.

By standing on a companion's shoulders, the tallest of the three was just able to reach the protective screen in the roof. The lock-down seals at each of the screen's four corners opened easily. According to the diagram they had just studied on the tiny display screen, this shield opened into a ventilation tube. Said tube executed several tight twists and turns before running down the section of the ship they desired to traverse.

Once the shield screen had been opened, the third Pandronian closed the door behind them and then climbed up onto his two companions and pulled himself into the tube above. Reaching down, he helped the first one, then the other into the shaft.

Turning in the cramped quarters, the last Pandronian to crawl in reached down to reseal the lock-downs from inside, using a small hand tool from his own pack to reach through the fine mesh to the locks on the outside.

Very soon thereafter, six armed security personnel turned down that same dead-end corridor in the course of scouring every possible avenue of escape. They moved to its end. With five phasers covering him, the ensign in charge tried first the door on the left. All instruments inside the little room appeared undisturbed and registering normally.

Then he turned to the door on the right. The room beyond was likewise deserted. "No sign of them." He turned to leave.

"Just a minute, sir," one of the crew said. "Shouldn't we check out that overhead vent?"

The ensign retraced his steps, leaned back to stare up at the uninformative grill overhead. "Could they have slipped in there?" He wondered aloud. "It doesn't seem likely, but we'd better make certain." He pulled out his communicator.

"Engineering?"

"Engineering. Lieutenant Markham here," came the crisp reply.

"This is Security Ensign Namura. We're hunting the Pandronian boarders, and just now I'm standing in ventilation operations cubicle"—he peered around at the open door—"twenty-six. There's a sealed ventilation shaft overhead. Could a man crawl through it?"

"Just a second, Ensign." There was a pause as the engineering officer ran the schematics for that region of the ship through his own viewscreen.

"Got it now. Several men or man-sized creatures might get up in there, but the shaft goes straight up for about four meters. Then it does a number of sharp doglegs to connect with other ventilation tubes before running into a main shaft. No way a man could get through those turns, not even a contortionist."

Namura moved, stared up into the dark tube above. "Hang on, Lieutenant." Removing a small device from his waist, the ensign activated it, sending a powerful if narrow beam of illumination upward. It lit the entire four vertical meters of shaft, which were manifestly empty.

"They're not up there. Thank you, sir," the ensign said, replacing the light at his hip and speaking again into his communicator. "Security team twelve out."

Shutting off his communicator, he directed his words to the other five. "They're not in here. Let's try the next service corridor down." Relaxing slightly, the group turned and trotted out of the subcorridor.

Contact by the average member of the crew with Pandronians or things Pandronian had been infrequent and rare. So it was unfortunately only natural that in his anxiety to run down three man-sized intruders, Namura had overlooked the basic nature of Pandronians, had not considered their physiological versatility. Far above and beyond the security team, in the very bowels of the *Enterprise*'s ventilation system, nine segments of three whole Pandronians made their rapid way around twists and turns which no man-sized creature could have negotiated.

An hour passed and a worried Uhura faced Communications. "Still no contact with the invaders, Lieutenant? It's been much too long."

"No, Lieutenant Uhurra," M'ress replied. If anything, she looked more haggard than her superior. Ears and whiskers drooped with exhaustion, her energy drained by the effort of coordinating dozens upon dozens of uninformative security reports from all over the ship, compounded by the tension which still gripped everyone on the bridge.

"Therre hasn't been a sighting of the Pandrronians in some time—only false rreporrts. One securrity team thought they had the boarrders trrapped nearr the Main Trransporrter Rroom, but they managed to slip past all purrsuerrs. I don't know what—"

Alarms suddenly began sounding at Communications, the command chair, and at several other stations around the bridge.

"Now what!" Uhura shouted.

Below, in another section of the cruiser, a badly dazed technician dragged himself to the nearest intercom. Acrid smoke swirled all around him, and the mists were lit by flashes of exploding circuitry and instrumentation shorting out. Phaser bolts and other energy beams passed through the choking air above and around him.

"Hello, hello!" he coughed into the pickup grid. "Bridge . . . emergency—"

"Bridge speaking; Lieutenant Uhura here. Who is this?"

"Technician Third Class Camus," the voice replied, shaky and barely discernible through the sounds of destruction around it. Something blew up close by and he was thrown slightly to one side. But one arm remained locked around the console containing the intercom. Bleeding from a gash across the forehead, he blinked blood from his eyes and coughed again.

"Camus—*Camus!*" Uhura yelled over the intercom. "What's your station? Where are you?"

"I'm . . . on . . . secondary bridge," he managed to gasp out. "We've been attacked. Only myself . . . two others on duty here. Standard maintenance compliment for ... area. Aliens attacked us ... slipped in before we knew what was happening. Must be ... the Pandronians." He blinked again.

"Can't see ... too well. Smoke. We didn't expect anything. Thought ... they were several decks above us."

"So did we," replied Uhura grimly. She glanced away, back toward Communications. "M'ress, notify all security teams that the Pandronians are attacking the secondary bridge." She turned her attention hastily back to the intercom.

"What happened, Mr. Camus?"

"Explosive charges ... not phasers. Shaped demolition, from what I can see." The smoke burned his eyes, and tears mixed with the blood from the gash above his eyes.

"Damage report?" Uhura queried.

"Helm's ... okay. So's most everything else, except for minor damage. But communications are completely gone. We were lucky ... I think."

"Report noted, Mr. Camus," Uhura told him. "This is important," she said slowly as something banged violently over the speaker. "Was the destruction achieved randomly or did they go for communications intentionally?"

"Don't know ... Lieutenant," the technician reported, trying to see around him. "Happened too fast to tell anything."

"Understood. Listen, if they're still there, try to tie them down with your phasers," Uhura ordered him. "Security teams are on their way to you."

"Will do, Lieutenant," the technician acknowledged, just before something touched him in the middle of his back and he slumped to the deck unconscious.

Uhura looked again at M'ress. "Direct all security teams in that area to block off all turbolifts and stairwells, seal all corridors near the secondary bridge. Maybe we can pin them down there. Also notify Sick Bay to send a medical team over—they've obviously experienced casualties." Her expression was not pleasant. "If any of those techs die, every phaser on this ship goes off stun."

There was a low murmur of agreement from the rest of the solemn bridge personnel. "Verry well, Lieutenant," the communications officer acknowledged.

"I also want extra security sent to Engineering at warp-drive control and at all approaches to the main bridge."

"Yes, Lieutenant."

Uhura voiced her thoughts aloud. "If they *were* trying for communications, or anything else on the secondary bridge, then their intentions are obvious. They're trying to cripple one or more ship functions. If that's the case, then I think they'll try for Engineering or the bridge next."

She leaned back in the command chair, resting a fist against one cheek and trying to make sense of what was going on. Several minutes passed and she noticed that the navigator had his eyes focused on her.

"Well, what are you looking at, Arex?" she snapped.

"I am as worried as you are, Lieutenant Uhura," the Edoan replied in his soft singsong voice.

"Staring at each other isn't going to help the situation any." The Edoan looked away, but remained deep in thought.

"I just can't help wondering why Pandronians, even the rebel Pandronians the captain mentioned, are trying so desperately to damage the *Enterprise*. They must know that three of them can't do any serious destruction, can't carry out anything we won't eventually repair." She shook her head slowly, wishing the solution were as simple as operating ship's communications . . . communications.

Apparently the same thought occurred to Arex. "If it is our communications they are trying to destroy," he theorized, "and not the ship itself, it seems to me there can be only one reason behind this. They are attempting to prevent us from keeping in touch with the landing party. Yet for them to want to do so must mean this rebellious faction knows the captain, Mr. Spock, and Dr. McCoy are, as they mentioned, aiding government forces. If that is the case—"

"If that's the case," an excited Uhura finished for him, "since only the Pandronian government knows we're helping them, that means that government is home to at least one traitor. The captain needs to be told."

"I believe the Pandronian government should also be notified," the always empathetic Edoan added.

"Lieutenant M'ress," Uhura began, "call the authorities in the Pandronian capital—anyone you can make contact with. Tell them it's vital for both their security and ours that we speak immediately to someone high up in the government. Then get in touch with the captain."

"Aye, aye," the tired Caitian replied. She turned back to her control console and prepared to carry out the orders.

She was interrupted by a loud thumping from somewhere across the bridge. Like everyone else, she paused, listening. Now the strange noise was the only sound on the bridge. It didn't remain stationary, but instead seemed to move from place to place. Abruptly, the noise ceased.

It was dead quiet for a minute, and then a loud bang sounded from overhead. "They're in the repair access space above us!" Uhura shouted.

"M'ress, emergency alert! Get a security team in here on the double. We've got to—"

Carrrumphh!

A powerful concussion shook the bridge. Smoke and haze filled the air, and nearly everyone was thrown to the deck. A hole had been blown in the roof, just to the right of the science station. Recovering well, everyone dove for cover in anticipation of the coming assault. Three sections of Pandronian dropped through the ragged gap, hurriedly assembled themselves into a complete assailant. Sections of a second came close behind, the three integrals joining together like midget acrobats.

As the second alien came together, the turbolift

doors to the bridge slid aside to reveal four battle-ready security personnel, phasers drawn and aimed outward.

Everything happened very quickly after that. Huddled behind the command chair, struggling for every breath, Uhura was able to absorb only isolated glimpses of the subsequent fight.

One Pandronian fired a burst at her from an unfamiliar weapon, which glanced harmlessly off the arm of the protective chair. The alien whirled quickly to fire at the turbolift. This second shot caught one of the charging security techs in the shoulder and sent her spinning to the deck.

Her companion slipped clear of the confines of the lift car and fired. The stun beam struck the first Pandronian in the midsection. As the alien collapsed, he came apart again. Ignoring the immobile midsection lying still on the deck, the head hopped onto the lower torso. One leg reached down, regained the weapon still held in a stiff hand, and prehensile toes commenced operating the gun as if nothing had happened.

The second, by now completely reformed Pandronian ignored the battle and raised a device whose muzzle was wider than its handgrip was long. He aimed it to Uhura's left and fired. The awkward-looking instrument emitted a dull *pop* which was barely audible over the noise and confusion swirling around the turbolift.

Luckily, M'ress had seen the alien point the weapon and had rolled aside. She escaped injury when the short, stubby missile landed in the middle of her console. For a microsecond the flare from Communications was too bright to look at directly. As it vanished, Uhura could see puffs of white smoke covering the console and surrounding instrumentation.

The Pandronian reloaded his weapon for a second shot. But by this time security personnel were pouring onto the bridge via walkways as well as the turbolift, faster than the three Pandronians could shoot them down.

Short and furious, the gun battle ended before the

second Pandronian could unload his second missile. It ended with all three aliens—or rather, all nine independently mobile sections of same—paralyzed and motionless on the floor.

When the last operative Pandronian integral, a furiously resisting head, had been stunned, Uhura, shaken, stood up from behind the command chair. One after another, the rest of the bridge complement rose or crawled out from their respective hiding places.

Only the security personnel who had resisted the attackers had been hit. Everyone else appeared healthy and able to resume his post. Security teams continued to pour onto the bridge, followed closely by medical teams responding to the emergency calls issued by the first to reach the bridge. It had grown incredibly crowded beneath the gap the attackers had blasted in the ceiling.

Uhura and Arex moved to examine the nine motionless shapes scattered across the deck. "Which one belongs to which one?" a bewildered security officer wondered.

"No telling," muttered Uhura. "Take the whole collection down. They can sort themselves out when they regain consciousness. When that happens, I've a few questions I want answers to—and I'll have them, or these three will be disassembled into a lot more than nine pieces!"

Under the close guard of a dozen security personnel, supervisory medical technicians loaded the various sections of dismembered aliens onto stretchers and carted them down to the security area of Sick Bay.

Once the bridge was clear of Security and Pandronians, Uhura used a pocket communicator to contact Engineering and request a repair team. Then she moved to stand before the shambles that had been the communications station.

M'ress met her there, trying to peer into the wreckage, yet careful to jerk clear whenever something within the white-hot mass would flare threateningly.

"I don't know what was in that missile," she confessed to Uhura, "but whateverr it was prroduced an enorrmous amount of heat. They couldn't have chosen a betterr way to make a thorrough mess of things."

It didn't take an expert to see what M'ress meant. Instead of being blown apart, the communications station had been melted, fused into a half-solid wall of metal and plastic slag. Where they could have replaced the damaged or destroyed areas resulting from an explosion, now the entire section of wall would have to be cut clear out to the depths of the heat damage and the console would have to be literally rebuilt.

When Scott heard what had happened, there was no holding him in Sick Bay, despite Chapel's admonitions. Having recovered the use of all but his legs below the knee the *Enterprise*'s chief engineer was on the bridge minutes later. He propped himself up on the mobile medical platform and directed the engineering team which had already commenced repairs. His steady swearing was directed at those who had dared violate his beloved equipment in so horrid a fashion.

It wasn't long before the subjects of Scotty's ire began to recover from the effects of security phasers. Uhura sat in the sealed security area and watched the activity within the Sick Bay cell as the Pandronians reassembled themselves.

"The lower portions recovered first, the head last," Chapel was explaining to her. "I expect that's only reasonable, since the heads contain the greatest concentration of nerves and would be most strongly affected by a phaser set on stun."

However, when Uhura began questioning them via a hand translator, the Pandronians might as well have remained unconscious, for all the loquaciousness they displayed.

"Why did you board the *Enterprise?*" she inquired for the twentieth time. All three sat quietly at the rear of the cell, ignoring the energy barrier and those beyond it while they stared with single-minded intensity at the back wall.

"Why did you destroy our communications facilities?"

Silence of a peculiarly alien kind.

"Was it to prevent our communicating with our landing party on Pandro? If so, how did you know about it?"

Perhaps, she thought, a question which should strike closer to home.

"Are you," she began deliberately, "connected to the rebel groups of Pandronians operating on Pandro? If that's true, why interfere with us? We have no desire to interfere in Pandronian domestic squabbles."

That was an outright lie, since the captain, Mr. Spock, and Dr. McCoy were openly aiding the present planetary government, but it produced the same response from the quiescent three, which was no response.

Uhura made a sound of disgust, turned to Chapel. "You're certain the paralysis has completely worn off?"

"From everything I can tell, they're fully functional. Any paralysis of the vocal apparatus is voluntary, Lieutenant."

"Fully functional, huh?" Uhura muttered sardonically. "Let's see some functioning, then." She raised her voice, all but screamed herself hoarse. "At least identify yourselves! Or are you going to insist you're not even Pandronians!"

Unexpectedly, the middle alien turned to face her. "We are the representatives of the True Order," he said contentedly.

Uhura was not impressed. "I seriously doubt that, whoever you are and whatever that's supposed to mean. But it's nice to know that you're capable of speech."

The Pandronian assumed a lofty pose. "Can talk to lower forms when mood occurs."

"Goody. Maybe you'd condescend to chat with this representative of a lower order about a few things. Once more: Why did you sneak aboard our ship?"

Dead silence. Uhura sighed.

"All right, if you don't want to talk about what you're doing here and why you've brutally assaulted those who mean you no harm, maybe you're willing to answer questions about yourselves." She began pacing back and forth in front of the energy barrier.

"What is this True Order you mentioned?"

"The Society of Right Integration," the Pandronian replied, as if talking to a child. "Only the True Order to restoring the natural order of lifes on Pandro is dedicated. Dedicated to bringing end to desecrating civilization now existing. Dedicated to eliminating vile government which perpetuates unnaturalness. To cleansing running sore of—"

"Take it easy," Uhura broke in. "You're giving me a running headache. What's this natural order you're so hot about restoring?"

Shifting his position slightly, the Pandronian gazed upward. "In beginning all lifes on planet Pandro had freedom of integration complete. Could integrate one life form with any other to achieve integrated shape pleasurable for moment or lifetimes. Had even primitive Pandronian intelligences like This One great flexibility of form. Often primitive rites including dividing and recombining to gain new insights into existences." The alien's voice turned from reverent to remorseful.

"Then did bastard civilization now grown huge begin to take hold. To become rigid, unfluid, frozen was Pandronian intelligences. Recombinations among intelligent Pandronians were," and his words became coated with distaste, "law forbidden. Realized only a few true believers, first of True Order, that this was horrible wrongness! Themselves dedicated to restoring naturalness of Pandronian lifes!"

His head dropped and turned resolutely from her. Further questions elicited only silence. Having delivered their sermon, the captives apparently had nothing more to say.

Uhura had listened stolidly to every word of the diatribe. Now, when it became clear they would learn nothing more from the three, she turned and spoke bitterly to Chapel.

"A bunch of religious fanatics. Wonderful! So somehow we've gotten ourselves mixed up in some kind of theological, philosophical rebellion against Pandronian society. A normal group of revolutionaries I'd know how to deal with, but these," and she gestured back at the silent Pandronians, "are of an impossible type anywhere in the galaxy. You can't talk reason and logic and common sense to them. Whatever such types are rebelling against is never worse than what they represent."

"I wonder," a concerned Chapel murmured, "if the captain and the others realize how fanatical their opposition is?"

"I don't know," Uhura muttered. "I hope so, because according to Chief Scott's preliminary estimation of the damage to ship's communication's facilities, we're certainly not going to be telling them about it for a while. Even energy-supplemented hand communicators would be hard pressed to reach the surface, assuming we could cannibalize enough components for them. And that kind of signal wouldn't get two centimeters through the radiation distortion now blanketing that region of the planet.

"I only hope the captain and Mr. Spock aren't as easily surprised as we were. . . ."

Once the strange roll-and-jolt novelty of riding the *zintar* had worn off, Kirk relaxed enough to enjoy their journey. One thing the ride never became was boring. Not with the incredible diversity of life that swarmed around them.

Kirk was able to study the constantly changing vista as the three *zintars* parted greenery and snarling animals alike, living ships plowing through waves of brown and green. In places he felt as if he recognized certain plants and, more infrequently, familiar animals that they had encountered before. As bn Bem had indicated earlier, these were the members of Pandronian nature which had found success and harmony in a particular combination of integrals. So much so that they reproduced as a continuing species.

These conservative representatives of Pandronian life were seemingly far outnumbered by the biologically unfulfilled. One could never predict what might hop, leap, run, or fly from behind the next tree, or scurry across a brief flare of open space ahead.

The excitement was intensified because the Pandronians were as new to many of these unstable shapes as Kirk. The thrill of never-ending discovery was intoxicating. In fact, he mused, that was the best way to describe the state of life on Pandro, where nature was on a perpetual drunk.

For the first time he had leisure to speculate on a host of related, equally fascinating possibilities. How, for example, did the Pandronians insure the stability of their domesticated animals? Imagine a farmer going out in the morning to milk the local version of a cow, only to find himself facing a barn full of bears.

Or what about mutating crops which could be nourishment incarnate when the sun went down and deadly poisonous on its rising? Even the stable forms of Pandronian life, like bn Bem and his ilk, were capable under proper stimulus of disassociating.

He didn't think, exciting as it was, that he'd care to be a Pandronian. Not when you could wake up one morning and find your head had gone for a walk.

Another full day and night of crashing through the undergrowth brought them to the end of the tracks. Dismounting from the lead *zintar,* the chief tracker confirmed that the *coryat* trail swung neither left nor right of the muddy, murky shoreline straight ahead, but instead vanished at the water's edge.

Perhaps coincidentally, the tracker also located evidence of considerable recent activity at that location on the shore, as of numerous creatures milling about in the soft soil where the tracks disappeared.

ab Af spoke to the *zintar* he was riding and the long furry form executed its elevator movement so that its riders could dismount easily.

McCoy was the first to approach the scum-laden edge of the water. "Not very appealing country," he commented, eyeing the unwholesome muck with professional distaste.

"An understatement, Doctor." McCoy turned, saw Spock standing just behind him and likewise surveying the terrain. "It is no wonder that the Pandronians have not ventured into it, or that eb Riss doubted Lieutenant Arex's information."

What lay before them was neither water nor mud, but something which partook of both qualities. Where it didn't eddy ponderously up against solid ground, the thick brownish sludge bubbled softly under the impetus of noisome subterranean gases. Delicate gray-green fungus floated over much of the shoreline shallows. It drifted and clung viscously to the boles of massive multirooted trees. Vines and creepers and things which might as easily have been animal instead of vegetable hung draped haphazardly from intertwined branches, forming a cellulose web above the waterways between the trees.

Noting the absence of screeches and screams, McCoy commented, "It's unusually quiet here, compared to the territory we've crossed." He walked back, questioned bn Bem. "Is it quieter here than in the forest because the swamps aren't as fertile?"

"No, McCoy Doctor," the commander assured him. "Swamp lifes strive noise not to make. Unhealthy to call attention to Oneself in swamplands." Kirk joined them, and bn Bem turned his attention to the captain.

"According to tracker ours and instruments yours, Kirk Captain, our quarry in there somewhere has gone." He made a broad gesture to encompass as much of the morass as possible. "Is still hard to believe any Pandronian would into swamplands flee, but seems so. To follow we must a raft build." He started to turn and walk away, but paused at a thought and looked back.

"Is *certain* your people found radiation source that way?" He pointed straight ahead into the depths of the stinking riot of growth.

Spock held out a confident arm, matching the direction of the commander's own. "Directly along this line, Commander."

"So it be, then," bn Bem agreed reluctantly. He faced eb Riss, "Set all to raft constructing. Must push and pull our way through. *Zintars* and handlers here will remain to await our return."

"What return?" eb Riss snorted resignedly. "In there to go is new death for all. Is madness to do, especially," and he glared haughtily at Kirk and Spock, "on word of outworlders."

"Forget you that *coryat* tracks lead here and signs of many creatures waiting disturb this place," bn Bem countered firmly. "Is advisable to go to source of strange radiation."

"Is not my objection to that," eb Riss corrected him. "Is getting to there from here my worry."

"On that I'm with you, Lud," McCoy commented, still studying the hostile nonground ahead of them. "Can't we just transport up to the ship and have Mr. Scott beam us down at the coordinates given for the radiation source, Jim?"

Kirk smiled apologetically. "You know that wouldn't be very good strategy, Bones. Remember the attitude of guards toward us when we first beamed down here with the commander? And they were expecting us. No, in this case slow but sure does the trick—I hope." He pulled out his communicator, flipped it open.

"But I don't think we'll have to fool with a raft." He glanced reassuringly at the curious bn Bem and eb Riss. "I'll order some strong folding boats sent down from ship's stores.

"Kirk to *Enterprise*." The normal brief pause between signal and reply came and passed. Frowning slightly, he tried again. "Kirk to *Enterprise* . . . come in, *Enterprise*." An arboreal creature squawked piercingly from somewhere behind them.

"Mr. Spock?" Kirk said, eyeing his first officer significantly. Spock activated his own communicator, repeated the call, and was rewarded with equal silence.

"Nothing, Captain. Nor is it radiation interference, this time. There is no indication that the ship is receiving our signals." He glanced over at bn Bem, who was watching anxiously.

"It would appear, Commander, that the rebel faction which we are tracking and which placed several of their number on board the *Enterprise* has managed to somehow interrupt ship-to-ground communications. Of course, we cannot yet be absolutely certain it is the same group, but evidence strongly points to it."

"I wonder if that's all they've managed to interrupt, Spock," McCoy grumbled.

"We've no way of knowing, Bones. And the breakdown could be due to other factors besides obstreperous Pandronians." McCoy could tell from the tone of Kirk's voice how little stock the captain placed in alternate possibilities. "We might as well proceed as sit here."

"To commence construction of the raft now," bn Bem directed eb Riss. The other Pandronian officer acknowledged the order and moved to comply.

Construction of two large rafts of local wood proceeded apace under eb Riss's skillful supervision. Kirk had to admit that the Pandronian, whatever his attitudes toward the Federation officers, knew what he was doing.

They were aided by the extreme mobility of the Pandronian troopers. Their ability to separate into two or three sections enabled each of them to perform functions no human could have duplicated, and with amazing speed.

As the day wore on they were attacked only twice while working on the rafts. According to bn Bem, this was an excellent average, considering their proximity to the teeming swamps. Kirk was thankful he wasn't present here on a day when the local life chose to act belligerently.

The first assault came when something like a large, supple tree trunk slithered out of the sludge nearby and panicked the Pandronians working nearest the shore. The creature sported long, branchlike tentacles. Its mimicry was lethally impressive: It looked exactly like a section of tree.

Under selective phaser fire from Kirk, Spock, and McCoy, the branches broke away, scampering in all directions on tiny legs to retreat back into the swamp and along the water's edge. Despite repeated phaser bursts, however, the main body of the tree snake remained where it had emerged from the muck, exhibiting no inclination to retreat.

Close inspection revealed the reason for this obstinacy. The thing didn't retreat because it couldn't. The trunk that looked like a tree was just that—an old warped log which the many small creatures that resembled branches had adopted as a central body.

"A poor choice of association," Spock commented. "Surely the branch animals could not hope to blend successfully with a vegetable."

"True is, Spock Commander," bn Bem agreed. "Is defensive integration for little long eaters. Other predators would be by size of this 'body' frightened off. Tomorrow will branch lifes be maybe spines on back of big carnivore, or maybe decorative striping along belly of big plant grazer."

The second attack on the raft builders was more insidious and dangerous than that of the almost pathetic branch imitators.

Kirk had gone for a stroll along the swamp edge, moving just deep enough into the forest to frustrate anything lurking below the sludge's surface. To snatch him from between these intertwining trees would require a Pandronian killer with more flexibility and brains than any Kirk had seen thus far.

He was taking care to remain within sight of the construction site when he heard the low thumping. It sounded something like a muffled shout.

Drawing his phaser, he moved cautiously forward, toward the source of the sound. In a partial clearing he discovered a rolling, jerking shape making frantic, nearly comprehensible noises. It was submerged under a blanket of olive-green puffballs. Two long ropes of interconnected puffballs were dragging the smothered form toward the ominous waterline nearby.

Kirk recognized that gesticulating, helpless shape immediately, was shouting back over a shoulder even as he ran forward.

"Spock—bn Bem—this way, hurry!"

Breaking into the clearing, he set his phaser for maximum stun and raised it toward the two living green ropes. At the same time he was assaulted by a horde of other fuzzy spheres. Not one was larger around than his fist. All were faceless, featureless. Other than the unbroken mantle of green fuzz, all that showed were three sets of tiny, jointed legs ending in a single short hooked claw.

Kirk experienced a moment of panic as the creatures swarmed around and onto him, began attaching themselves to his legs and feet. There was no pain, no biting sensation from unseen jaws. The puffballs neither stuck nor clawed nor punctured his skin, but merely grabbed tight and held on.

A similar multitude had blanketed McCoy to the point where only the doctor's hands, lower legs, and face remained visible. He was using all his strength to keep the fuzzy spheres clear of his mouth, nose, and eyes, so that he could still see and breathe. Every time he opened his mouth to call for help, one of the puffballs rolled over it, and he had to fight to clear the orifice. Meanwhile, the two long lines of interlocked balls, like knotted green hemp, continued to drag the doctor ever closer to the shore.

Kirk's phaser, carefully aimed, cleared some of them off his own arms and McCoy's body, but even as dozens fell stunned, other newcomers swarmed out of the underbrush to take their place. In seconds, however, Spock, bn Bem, and several Pandronian soldiers had joined him. With the addition of Spock's phaser, they were able to keep the fuzzy reinforcements at bay.

bn Bem and the soldiers were rushing toward the trapped McCoy. Each Pandronian brandished a long prod ending in a hypodermic tip. Working smoothly and efficiently, they began poking each individual bristle ball with the needles. Kirk learned later what he was too busy then to guess—each poke injected a puffball with a minute quantity of the same drug that the *fasir's* syringe darts carried.

bn Bem and his companions began at the spot where the twin chains of green were holding on to McCoy. As soon as one ball fell away, another rushed in to take its place and continue the seemingly inexorable march toward the swamp.

But with Kirk and Spock now holding all reinforcements at the edge of the forest clearing, re-formation of the two green chains took longer and longer. Finally the chain was permanently broken and the Pandronians were able to begin picking individual puffballs off McCoy. When that was concluded, they chased the remaining spheres into the depths of the forest.

"You okay, Bones?" Kirk asked solicitously as he hurried over to the doctor. McCoy was sitting up, slightly groggy, and brushing at his clothing where the tiny creatures had clung.

"I guess so, Jim. They didn't break the skin or anything."

"How did it happen, Doctor?" asked Spock.

McCoy considered a moment before replying. "I was bending to get a closer look at something that looked like an overgrown aboveground truffle over"—he abruptly began searching around, finally pointing toward a tree deeper in the forest—"over there. Then it felt like someone had dumped a hundred-kilo bale of hay on me.

"Next thing I knew I was rolling over on the ground while those little monstrosities poured over me." He kicked at a couple of the immobile, now innocent-looking green balls.

"They were all over me in an instant. And they won't be pulled off." As Kirk helped him to his feet McCoy queried the commander, "What are they, anyhow?" His face contorted irritably and he resumed rubbing at his clothes. "They may not bite, but they sure itch like the devil."

"*Vigroon*," bn Bem replied, nudging several of the olive globes with a blue foot. "A successful life form we well know. Even near Tendrazin we have them, but they are not dangerous generally, since occur not nearly in such impressive numbers.

"By selves are harmless eaters of insect forms and other small things. But in integration they act concerted—as you have had opportunity to observe, McCoy Doctor."

"Saints preserve me from such opportunities," McCoy mumbled, trying to scratch a place on his back he couldn't reach.

"Are found near water only, when in dangerous numbers," bn Bem went on helpfully. Kneeling, he pushed six legs and fur aside on one of the immobile *vigroon,* to reveal a tiny circular mouth lined with minute teeth.

"Single, even fair number of *vigroon* could not kill any animal of size. Jaws too small and weak, teeth too tiny. But in large number integration can associative *vigroon* smother large prey or drown it. Last named what they try to do to you, McCoy Doctor.

"Many *vigroon* jump on prey creature to keep it from fleeing. Others link up to pull into water, where held under until drowned. Can then devour nonresisting corpse at their leisure. You would a great feast have been for them, McCoy Doctor."

"Thanks, but I don't feel complimented," McCoy muttered in response to the commander's evaluation.

"You sure you're not hurt, Bones?"

"I'm fine, Jim. Even the itching's beginning to fade—thank goodness."

Kirk turned to his first officer. "Mr. Spock, try to raise the *Enterprise* again."

"Very well, Captain." Activating his communicator, Spock attempted to contact the ship, with the same results as before.

"Still no response whatsoever, sir."

Kirk sighed, sat down on a rock, and ran both hands through his hair. "Things happen awfully fast with Pandronians. I still haven't figured out how those rebels managed to board the ship, not to mention knock out our communications. Pandronian technology just isn't supposed to be that advanced."

"We admit to knowing little about Pandro, Captain. It is conceivable that our preliminary fleet reports understated their achievements in certain areas by several factors. Given what has taken place so far, it would seem more than merely conceivable—unless another explanation can be found."

Kirk glanced up hopefully. "Have you any alternative in mind, Mr. Spock?"

The first officer managed to appear discouraged. "I regret, Captain, that I do not."

VIII

From the moment the two rafts were launched into the murky water Kirk could sense nervousness in the Pandronian troops. As they poled and paddled their way clear of the shore, the nervousness increased—and there was nothing more unnerving than watching a Pandronian with the jitters, their heads shifting position on their shoulders with startling unpredictability.

Kirk could sympathize. There was no telling what might lurk just beneath the surface of a swamp on any world, and on Pandro that was true a thousand times over. But as they traveled farther and deeper into the seemingly endless morass of sweating trees and dark waters and nothing monstrous arose to sweep the rafts out from beneath them, the Pandronians gained confidence. Oddly, though, the more relaxed and assured the regular troops became, the more concerned and uncertain grew Commander Ari bn Bem.

Kirk was finally moved to ask what was the matter. "Why the nervous face, Commander? We've had no trouble so far—less than we had when we were 'safely' on shore building the rafts." He peered into the dank mists ahead. "I don't see any sign of trouble, either."

"Is precisely what worries This One, Kirk Captain," bn Bem told him softly. "Should we have been assailed by unwholesome lifes several times by now. Not only has that happened not, but is little sign of any kinds of lifes, antagonistic or otherwise.

"In fact, the deeper into *varbox* we go, the scarcer

becomes all life forms. Is strange. Is worrisome. Is most unsettling."

"Is it possible," Spock ventured, "that the rebellious Pandronians, who presumably have retreated through here on many occasions, could have committed so much destruction and taken so much life that the surviving inhabitants of this region have fled to other sections of the swamp?"

"Would take army of Pandronians all equipped with *fasirs* to clear even tiny portion of *varbox*," the commander countered, "and then would suffer heavy casualties in process. Would not think Mad Ones had such power or abilities at their command. If so, would believe they would have caused Pandro government much more trouble than they have before now. Find possibility unworkable, Spock Commander," he concluded firmly.

"Can you offer an alternate explanation for the comparative tranquillity of our passage, then?" the first officer wanted to know.

bn Bem openly admitted he could not. He repeated his feelings again: "Worries me."

Lud eb Riss, who was in command of the second raft poling alongside them, didn't share the commander's paranoia. "I see not why it should," he exclaimed almost happily. "Lucky can These Ones count themselves. Personal opinion This One is that if we not another meat-eater see again, will be more than pleased. Not to look gift *zintar* in the masticatory orifice."

They made excellent, unimpeded progress through the *varbox* all that day. When it grew too dark to travel accurately, they camped on the rafts for the night, mooring them to each other and to four great trees. The thick boles formed a rough square, and their net of vines and creepers provided a psychologically pleasing barrier overhead.

Soft hootings and muted howls colored the night, but none of them came close enough to trouble the sleepers or the Pandronian troops on guard duty. Except for the humidity, the following morning was almost pleasant.

"When do we reach this place by your ship's supposedly infallible instruments located, Kirk Captain?" an irritable eb Riss wanted to know when the morning had passed.

Kirk turned to his first officer. "Well, Mr. Spock?"

Spock frowned slightly, his attention shifting from the view forward to the figure-covered sketch he held in one hand. "We should have reached it already, Captain. I confess to being somewhat discouraged, but we may still—"

A loud Pandronian shout caused him to break off and, along with everyone else, look ahead. The second raft was moving a little in advance of the other, and a sharp-eyed trooper standing precariously on the foremost log was chattering excitedly in Pandronian. bn Bem and eb Riss were both straining to see something no one else had.

Kirk, Spock, and McCoy did likewise, and the reason for the lookout's enthusiasm became evident seconds later. They were once more nearing solid land. It rose in a smooth, firm bank from the sludge's edge. Despite the thick cover of growth, there was no concealing it. The ground looked as solid as that they had left the long Pandronian day before.

"I thought you once mentioned, Commander," Spock murmured, "that the width and length of this swampland was far greater than this."

"So This One did," bn Bem replied positively. "And so it is." He gestured at the muddy beach they were approaching. "Cannot possibly be other side of *varbox*. Can only one thing be: an island in *varbox* middle."

"But you cannot be certain?" the first officer persisted.

bn Bem turned to face him. "Cannot, since no Pandronian has ever penetrated into *varbox* this far—and returned to tell about it. But can be ninety-eight percent positive is *not* other side of *varbox*. Island must be. Could be many others."

"We can count at some future date," Kirk interrupted them. "Right now I'm interested in finding out what's on this particular one."

"Is seconding feelings, Kirk Captain," said bn Bem

fervently, his hand fondling the dark sidearm strapped to his hip.

Both rafts grounded on the muck of the narrow beach. Amid much grunting and struggling by Pandronians and Federation officers alike, the waterlogged rafts were pulled far enough up onto the mud-cum-earth to insure their not drifting away. Probably they needn't have bothered with the effort, since the current here was nearly nonexistent.

No one, however, wanted to chance being marooned in the center of the dismal region without an immediate means of retreat. If the island turned out to be small, there might not be enough suitable lumber present to duplicate the rafts.

But as they moved cautiously inland it became slowly apparent that the island they trod was one of respectable size, despite the difficulties of seeing very far to either side because of the dense ground cover. Had it not been for bn Bem's and eb Riss's assurance that they could not possibly have traversed the entire swamp, Kirk would have felt certain they had landed on its opposite shore.

Gradually the trees gave way to brush and thick bushes, the jungle turning reluctantly into less dense savanna. It appeared they might even be entering an open area, like a grassy plain. The low, easily ascendable hill looming ahead of them was almost barren of growth. Only a few scraggly bushes poked forlorn stems above the waving pseudograss.

"We ought to be able to get a good look at the rest of the island from up there," Kirk surmised, indicating the low summit. "This can't be a very high island. Not if the *varbox* maintains its similarity to Terran swamplands."

Starting forward, he pushed aside several bare branches and took a step upward.

The hill moved.

Jumping clear, Kirk joined the rest of the party in retreating back toward the jungle. Disturbed, the hill continued to quiver and rise heavenward.

"*Nightmare!*" bn Bem shouted in Pandronian. But

Kirk felt he could translate the commander's exclamation without resorting to instruments.

At full extension the apparition was at least ten meters tall, equally wide. As to how long it actually was they had no way of telling, because they couldn't see around the thing.

A minimum of twelve heads glared down at them. Each head was different from the next, no two alike, boasting various numbers of eyes and nostrils and ears. Each mouth save one (which showed a round sucker at its end) displayed varying but impressive stores of cutlery.

Each head bobbed and twisted at the end of a different neck. Some were long and snakelike, others short and heavily armored. Still others were jointed like a long finger. Several of the "growths" Kirk had noted on the creature's side and top moved independently, along with limbs of all shapes and sizes scattered seemingly at random along both sides of the horrible mass.

Grossest abomination of all was the huge body itself, a bloated ellipsoid whose skin alternated from feathers to scales to a smooth, pebbled epidermis not unlike the surface of certain starships. The skin was squared in places, round in others, concave in still more.

It looked as if something had taken a cargoload of creatures and thrown them into a vast kettle, then pounded and boiled the entire collection together and somehow reanimated the ghastly concoction. As the thing moved, the most awful cacophony of whistles, tweets, howls, and bellows issued from the various mouths. Round eyes big as a man glared down from one skull, flanked by slitted pupils in a second. One great burning red crescent shone in the midst of a third.

Somehow the beast moved, on an assortment of limbs as diverse as the rest of it. Short, thick pseudopods alternated with stubby, thick-nailed feet and long-clawed running limbs. It humped rather than walked toward them.

Still retreating into the jungle, the Pandronians fought to assemble their *fasir*. With phasers set on maximum, Kirk, Spock, and McCoy blasted away at the oncoming behemoth. It was like trying to stop a three-dimensional phalanx instead of a single creature.

Various sections and integrals would drop away—injured or killed—but the undisciplined collage would retain its shape and purpose. One, two, three heads were sliced away by the powerful handguns. The remaining nine continued to dart and probe for prey as if nothing had happened.

The Pandronians had almost assembled the dart-thrower when a high whining sounded. Every Pandronian, from the lowest-ranking soldier up to bn Bem, abruptly fell to the ground. They lay there, moaning and holding their heads.

Completely unaffected, a dumbfounded trio of Federation officers stood nearby, uncertain whether to aid their fallen allies or to continue firing at the lumbering mountain in front of them.

Events decided for them. As the first whine sounded, the creature's dreadful roars and yowls turned into a pitiable assortment of mewings and meeps and cries of pain. It turned like a great machine and began flopping off gruesomely toward the south, smashing down vegetation as it went until it had passed from sight.

Once the beast had vanished, the sound stopped.

When no explanation for this fortunate but inexplicable occurrence presented itself, Kirk turned his attention to something hopefully more understandable.

"What happened to the Pandronians, Bones?"

McCoy looked up at him. He was bending over one of the soldiers. "Beats me, Jim. The sound that drove off that grotesque impossibility also hit them pretty hard. Don't ask me why, or what produced it."

The soldier's normal healthy blue color had faded drastically. Every other Pandronian had similarly paled, though now their normal hue began to return.

"Inside my head, suddenly something," a panting bn Bem told them. "Painful, but more shock than anything else, This One thinks. Could tolerate if had to, but would rather not."

"From the look on your face, I can understand

why," a sympathetic McCoy agreed. "What felled you drove off the monster as well. I suppose we should be grateful for that, but somehow I'm not so sure. At best this was a pretty indiscriminate kind of rescue."

"I do not think that term is entirely appropriate, under the circumstances," a voice objected. Everyone turned to its source.

Standing in a slight gap in the undergrowth leading toward the center of the island stood a semicircle of Pandronians. Kirk experienced no elation at the sight of their black robes and hoods. They wanted their suspicions about the Pandronian rebels confirmed, but not under these conditions.

More important even than the presence of Pandronian rebels here deep in the *varbox* were the modern hand weapons they held trained on the government party. They differed noticeably in their sophistication from anything Kirk had seen on Pandro so far. He almost recognized them—no, he *did* recognize them.

The source of the weapons—and probably the explanation for a great many other as yet unexplained occurrences—was to be found in the middle of the Pandronians: one, two . . . three Klingons.

Holstering his own sidearm, the one in the middle walked forward, stopped an arm's length from Kirk. "Captain James Kirk, I presume? I am Captain Kor of the Imperial Science Division. You and your companions—he gestured to include the dazed Pandronians as well as Spock and McCoy—"are my prisoners."

"What's the meaning of your presence here, Kor?" Kirk snapped, unintimidated. "What are you up to on this world?"

"You will probably find out in due course, Captain," Kor assured him. "Until then, I require your sidearm, please?" He held out a hand for the gun in Kirk's fist.

Kirk studied the surrounding group, all armed with Klingon weapons, and then reluctantly handed over his phaser. Spock and McCoy followed.

Black-clad Pandronians immediately ran toward them, disarming their counterparts and confiscating anything resembling a weapon, including the partially assembled *fasir*.

Under close guard, the helpless group started into the island's interior.

"Actually," Kor said imperiously, "you should all thank me for saving your lives. Had I not ordered the controller activated, the creature would likely have exterminated you by now."

"Not true," protested bn Bem with dignity. "*Fasir* would have induced deintegration in monster."

"Perhaps," Kor admitted, showing white teeth in a wide grin. "Primitive though they are, your local weapons are effective, in their fashion. And the creature was, after all, only one of our more modest experiments."

"Experiments?" echoed a curious Spock.

"First and Science Officer Spock," Kirk said tightly, "and this is our ship's chief physician, Dr. McCoy."

Kor did not acknowledge the introductions. After all, the officers were prisoners. "Experiments," he conceded, "yes. Experiments which it has been your misfortune and our inconvenience for you to have stumbled upon, Captain Kirk. Why could you not simply have returned to your ship and taken your trouble-making selves elsewhere?"

"I don't know about the misfortune part," Kirk replied, glaring as a black-clad Pandronian prodded him with the muzzle of a weapon, "but you can bet on the inconvenience. The presence of armed Klingons on a world of high sentience like Pandro, without the knowledge and consent of the Pandronian government, is strictly forbidden by all Federation-Klingon treaties. Your presence here constitutes a violation of the most serious order, Captain Kor."

"No doubt certain parties would consider it so," the Klingon captain replied, "if it were ever to come to their attention." His grin turned predatory. "But that will not happen. And besides," he added, affecting an attitude of mock outrage, "we are *not* here without the Pandronians' permission."

"I beg to differ," said Spock. "No one in the government mentioned anything to us about the presence of a Klingon mission on Pandro. They surely would have."

"Can be of that certain," bn Bem finished.

"That depends on who you chose to recognize as the official government, Mr. Spock," Kor pointed out pleasantly. "We happen to feel that these representatives of a free society are the legitimate representatives of the Pandronian people." He indicated the black-clad figures escorting them. "Not the illegitimate government which has its seat in the city of Tendrazin."

"Government has support of overwhelming majority of Pandronian people," an angry bn Bem protested.

"A question of figures—mere quibbling," countered Kor, obviously enjoying himself.

"How do you have the gall to call these rebels a legitimate government?" Kirk demanded to know.

"They are for free disassociation and reassociation of all Pandronian life," the Klingon explained.

bn Bem could not longer contain himself. "Means destruction of civilization!" he shouted. "Would These Mad Ones destroy all civilization on planet Pandro by having intelligent Pandronians return to unordered integrals!"

"Anarchy," Spock concurred, "would be the undeniable result." He quieted when one of the Klingons gestured warningly with his gun.

Kirk suddenly looked thoughtful. "A lot of things are becoming clear now. How the rebels managed to simulate our communicator signals and get themselves beamed aboard the *Enterprise,* for example. And if they were responsible for the breakdown of communications between the ship and ourselves, how they knew where to go and what to destroy. Klingons were helping them every step of the way." He glared at Kor.

"I would be unduly modest if I denied aiding these brave Pandronian patriots," the captain confessed. "When you do not return to your ship, Captain Kirk, your death will be attributed to the malignant Pandronian swamp life—which will in fact be the truth." Kirk didn't like the sound of that one bit.

"It is hoped," Kor continued, "that the *Enterprise*

will accept that information, along with your bodies, and leave Pandro orbit."

"You don't know Scotty," Kirk warned him.

"Scotty?" The Klingon looked puzzled.

"My current officer-in-charge. He's not the kind to gracefully accept three corpses without a more detailed explanation of how they came to be that way."

"Our explanation will be sufficient, Captain," Kor assured him. "We will concoct something so reasonable, so logical, that even the most skeptical mind will accept it. The story will have the advantage that none of you three or any of these misguided Pandronians," and he indicated bn Bem and the soldiers, "will be in a position to refute it."

"If you want us dead," Spock asked, obviously confused, "why didn't you allow that creature to kill us when it had the chance?"

"A couple of good reasons," Kor replied readily. "First, the possibility did exist that the Pandronians' *fasir* might have caused the creature to permanently disassociate. We do not like our expensive experiments ruined, not even the small ones."

"Small one," McCoy muttered.

"It was still a viable subject for further experimentation," the Klingon continued, "and therefore valuable to us. More important, we could not have permitted the destruction of our most valuable Pandronian operative."

Kirk stumbled, saw that bn Bem was too shocked even for that. "Valuable operative? Are you saying . . . ?"

"It would appear," Spock said, looking around carefully, "that our good friend Lub eb Riss has gone elsewhere."

bn Bem uttered a long string of Pandronian curses.

"The good eb Riss," Kor informed them, "is already ahead of us, on his way to our headquarters building. He has kept with him a small, supremely efficient Imperial communicator. With this we have easily been kept apprised of your progress." The Klingon shook his head sadly.

"You should have followed his advice to turn back instead of entering the *varbox*. He did his best to dissuade you, but you fools wouldn't listen. It would have spared me some awkwardness, not to mention what it would have spared you." He sniffed.

"However, you are here. So now you must be disposed of, and in a manner to satisfy your Mr. Scotty and everyone else on the *Enterprise*, Captain Kirk."

Another several dozen meters and the brush vanished entirely, revealing a cluster of fairly large prefabricated structures of Klingon style. Despite the speed with which they had clearly been put together, the buildings conveyed an impression of solidity. Multiple antennae bristled above one structure. Kirk also took note of what appeared to be a barracks for Klingon regulars and a series of interconnected science labs.

Ample use of local vegetation had been made, and the buildings gave every indication of being well camouflaged from the air. Off to the left, across a grassy open space, light danced and flared, indicating the presence of extremely powerful energy barriers— the partial source, at least, of the radiation that had so engaged the attention and curiosity of Lieutenant Arex.

"What do you keep on the other side of those fields?" Spock inquired, nodding in their direction.

"Our important experimental subjects, of course," Kor responded. "You will have an opportunity to see them at close range before too long—under unfavorable circumstances, I fear." He looked toward the swirling, shifting barrier. "At the moment they are all down toward the far end of the island. They prefer to stay as far away from the controller as possible."

"You mentioned this controller before," McCoy reminded him.

"Yes. It is the device which produced the frequency that drove your attacker away," Kor explained, "and incidentally stunned your Pandronian friends. Our true-thinking Pandronians," and he again pointed to the silent rebels around them, "are provided by us with special devices that fit over the head and cancel out the frequency. We have located one, you see, which causes considerable discomfort to all Pandronian life forms."

"Monsters you are," bn Bem growled. "Will never the Klingon Empire now bring Pandro under its influence. Ourselves will align with the Federation."

bn Bem's declaration constituted a Pyrrhic victory at best, Kirk knew, since it was growing more and more unlikely the commander would be able return to Tendrazin to convey his recommendations to the government. Kor's threats were hardly idle. Given the severity of the treaty violation represented by this installation's presence on Pandro, he couldn't chance releasing any of them alive. That had been self-evident from the moment Kirk had identified him as a Klingon, back near the jungle's edge.

"But what's your purpose behind all this?" he asked, indicating the extensive illegal station. "Why are you risking so much to carry out a few experiments? Or are you going to let these rebels use your frequency modulator to attack Tendrazin?"

"Certainly not," Kor insisted. "That would be dangerous to us, as well as unnecessary. For one thing, our rebel friends don't really have the expertise required to operate such advanced equipment as the controller. For another, its widespread use could be easily detected by any off-world observer. The Pandronians themselves would know immediately that the device was not developed on Pandro, and could notify any number of nosy busybodies."

"The Organians, for example?" suggested McCoy.

"There are certain parties," Kor admitted, "that might frown on such aid to one group of dissidents on an independent world. And there *is* that awkward treaty you mentioned, Captain Kirk. No, the controller is not a subtle weapon. And strong-willed Pandronians could resist it enough to fight back. Our friends are still few in number."

"Is clear now," a slightly subdued bn Bem observed. "They seek the collapse of our society for their own ends."

"Everything suddenly makes sense," Spock agreed.

"The rebels destroy the present Pandronian government and take over, thus instigating a massive wave of disassociation among the planet's sole intelligent species. The Klingons, who are waiting on the sidelines, promptly step in, declare themselves selfless benefactors, and commence restoring Klingon order amid the chaos they themselves have helped to bring about." He reached for his translator, eyed Kor expectantly. But the confident Klingon captain offered no objection to Spock's use of the instrument.

Turning to the nearest black form, the first officer more or less repeated what he had just said, concluded by saying, "I am surprised you Pandronian rebels, whatever your personal beliefs, do not realize this."

"We assurances have," the Pandronian replied, "that once present unnatural government of Pandro is broken, Klingons will leave us in free disassociation. We only need permit them to establish base or two and count planet Pandro among their worlds of influence."

"If they go back on their promise to you," Spock argued, "you'll have no effective government with which to oppose them."

The Pandronian made his equivalent of a shrug. "Is disassociation and return to natural order that important is most. All else incidental is."

Spock gave up. "Rousseauian philosophy carried to a dangerous extreme, Captain."

"Mad," was bn Bem's evaluation. "All are mad."

"You will be properly dealt with soon enough, Captain Kirk," Kor told him. "But there is no great hurry, and as you have expressed an interest in our experiments here, and as to how we intend to aid our rebel associates, I see no reason why you should not go to your extinction well educated." He drew out a small control device.

"This remote is locked into the large controller inside the installation. It is convenient to be able to work out in the open, especially since our more successful experiments could never fit inside. Let's see"—he gazed down the wall of energy on their left—"I think the nearest cell will be most appropriate. The barrier also splits into individual cells for different experiments, you see."

He adjusted controls on the small box. Again the whine they had heard earlier sounded, but it was not as intense this time.

"It is now a bad headache like," bn Bem complained, wincing noticeably.

"It will get worse," Kor told him without a trace of compassion. "The various broadcast units are already operating full strength at the other end of the island, thus driving the creature toward us instead of away."

McCoy was staring intently through the energy barrier. "I don't see anything."

"Patience, Dr. McCoy," Kor advised him. "It is a large island, and the objects of our experiments must have room to move about freely."

They continued to wait in expectant silence. Except for a few intermittent flashes of fire across its fabric, the energy barrier was perfectly transparent. Most of the time there seemed to be nothing there at all, but Kirk knew that if he walked forward he would eventually encounter an invisible wall capable of stopping much more than a lone man.

As promised, the whining grew stronger, until bn Bem and the other Pandronian soldiers were once again writhing in pain. Captain Kor coldly ignored them and turned a deaf ear to McCoy's entreaties.

"Ah, it approaches. One of our noblest products to date, Captain Kirk."

"Something is certainly coming toward us, Captain," Spock announced, staring off into the distance.

Totally awed, they all gazed openmouthed as the living mountain moved toward the barrier. It dwarfed the monstrosity which had attacked them on landing at the island, made it appear a newborn puppy by comparison. Nearer it came, nearer, until it seemed it couldn't be any larger. And yet there was more of it behind.

Kirk forced himself not to flinch as the colossus halted on the other side of the barrier barely five meters away.

"We are quite safe," Kor told them. "There is a

double barrier, one inside the other, in case by some unlikely mischance one should fail. Each is quite able to restrain such creatures. We take no chances with our experiments, you see."

Gazing up and up at the gargantuan thing, Kirk could understand why. It was hard to believe the mountain was alive. It was easily a hundred meters high and at least twice that in length. Comparing it again to the monster that had attacked them earlier found that smaller beast a model of symmetry compared to this thing. At least it had faintly resembled an organized creature. This sported head and necks in no special place or order. Only the legs appeared even vaguely arranged according to natural law. From time to time new eyes or ears or mouth orifices would appear along the rolling, quivering flanks, while other organs would vanish within. The creatures apparently existed in a continual state of reintegration and disassembly.

"An impressive mass," Kor observed rhetorically. "It weighs many thousands of qons." There was an evil pride in his voice as he enumerated the virtues of his crime against nature.

"This is the most mobile one of its size we have been able to produce, although the barrier restrains some much larger but not nearly so agile."

"How," McCoy wondered, staring up at the burbling mountain, "did you succeed in getting so many small integrals to combine into such a monstrosity? Even Pandronian nature operates according to some laws."

"It is a forced, artificially induced association, of course," Kor explained. "The integration is accomplished by employing a combination of controller frequencies and a hormone we have synthesized. The hormone is essentially the antithesis of that used by the Pandronians in their weapons, such as the *fasir*. That drug forces Pandronian life forms to disassociate, while our chemical impels them irresistibly to associate, to combine into larger, ever larger forms."

"It's still impossible," McCoy insisted. "How could something that big feed itself?"

"To begin with," Kor told him, "it is basically carnivorous. You can tell that from the preponderance of teeth and claws. Such a mass would ravage this entire swampland quickly enough, would eat its way across an entire planet in short order. We synthesize enough raw protein to keep our experiments like this one satiated. Of course, when we eventually succeed in developing a creature with high mobility, it will support itself when necessary."

"I would still know your purpose behind this," Spock said quietly.

"Oh, come now, Mr. Spock. I expect better of a Federation science officer. The universe is full of weapons. Not all need to be inorganic. A creature of this size," he went on as the experiment in question began to pound with awesome but silent futility against the inner force screen, "could assault a position defended even by phaser cannon. Because when one small portion of itself is destroyed, the rest continues on, thanks to its individual integrals.

"One would need to concentrate an enormous amount of firepower on it to reduce it to sizes susceptible to hand-weapon fire. By that time the creature would already have overwhelmed any field position, no matter how well emplaced and defended. The controller would see to that."

"Impractical," Kirk snapped. "Transporting several such monsters to a world in combat would be an impossible problem in logistics."

"Not at all," Kor countered. "We simply use the Pandronians own disassociation drug—in a diluted formula—thus causing the creature to disassemble into manageable sizes. These will then be transported like any breakdown weapon to the world in question and there reassembled on the battlefield through the use of the integrator hormone and the controller.

"Naturally," the Klingon captain added after a moment's pause, "not everything is perfected as yet. The problem of high mobility, for example. But do not worry—perfection is not far off. When that comes, Pandro will be turned into an organic arsenal for the Empire!"

IX

"What," Spock inquired as they were being led toward the nearest building, "do your Pandronian allies think of your plans?"

Kor showed no hesitation in replying. "The brave Pandronians who have chosen our assistance to aid them in their struggle against the repressive autocrats of Tendrazin care nothing for what we might wish to do in the swamplands, provided we permit free association and disassociation among intelligent beings on Pandro. They know that the results of our experiments will be utilized on other worlds, not here."

Kirk tried to imagine the colossus thundering against the impenetrable barrier before them let loose on a mechanized battlefield, or dropped into the center of a large city whose inhabitants might elect to resist Klingon rule—and he shuddered.

"The reb—patriots," Kor continued, "have granted us full permission to make use of all the Pandronian lower life we require for our experiments."

"You're not going to use the frequency modulator, you're not going to unleash your abominations on this world, and yet you say you're going to help the rebels topple the government without using Imperial weaponry. I'd like to know how," Kirk wondered.

"The Pandronian government will fall of its own accord, rotten as it is," Kor announced solemnly.

"You mean, unhelpful to Klingon as it is, don't you?" said McCoy angrily.

"Actually," the Klingon captain added in less pontifical tones, "it will collapse because we aided the rebels in one slight sortie."

"The theft of the Tam Paupa—so that's how this motley assortment of fanatics managed to pull that off."

"You malign our patriots," commented a disapproving Kor. "Nevertheless, it is here. Would you like to see it?"

"The Tam Paupa ... it here is?" a reverent bn Bem whispered, his head ringing.

"Would I lie to you?" grinned Kor.

"Would a Klingon—" McCoy began, but he was restrained by Spock. Why he couldn't have his say he didn't know, since they were going to be killed anyway; but Spock always had good reasons for employing physical restraint. The comment died aborning.

"Inside, please," Kor commanded them. They entered the building.

bn Bem expressed relief. "They have turned off the controller, This One thinks."

"I still can't believe you haven't used heavy weapons on Pandro, in contravention of still another treaty point," Kirk essayed. "How do you keep the dangerous swamp life clear of your pathway through the *varbox,* not to mention off this island?"

"That's no problem, Captain Kirk. Consider the modest experiment you encountered just inland. We let a few that size roam more or less freely about the perimeter of the island, and run some back and forth through the swamp path we've chosen with the use of controller remotes like this one." He tapped the control box at his waist.

"Most Pandronian life gladly makes haste to other regions. Those that do not help by reducing somewhat our need to produce synthesized protein." He smiled wolfishly.

"By the way, Mr. Spock, I know that you've had your communicator on open broadcast since we captured you." The first officer stiffened slightly. "It is of no consequence. Your unit could not penetrate the radiant screening around this installation. Even if it could, our operatives on board the *Enterprise* have evidently accomplished their task of disrupting your ship's communications equipment.

"By the time they have ship-to-surface capability restored, you will not be around to signal for beam-up. But your communicators will, so that you can be beamed back aboard—what's left of you, that is. I might point out that the modern weaponry which so concerns you, Captain Kirk, still has not been used on Pandro—but only on the *Enterprise*."

He pushed through a door leading into a busy lobby. Variously uniformed Klingons mixed freely with black-clad Pandronians. "Before too long the absence of the Tam Paupa will begin to make itself felt in government circles. Soon word of its absence will breach government security and spread to the general populace.

"Panic will ensue. The government will be in complete disarray. The Pandronians' natural bellicosity will come to the fore and *cusim*—no more planetary government."

The group halted at the end of the lobby, where Commander bn Bem and the other Pandronian soldiers were separated from Kirk, Spock, and McCoy.

"If not meet again, Kirk Captain," bn Bem murmured softly, "was for This One good to have known you. For you sentiments same, Spock Commander, McCoy Doctor."

The Pandronians were led away, while the *Enterprise* officers were taken down a nearby narrow corridor. At its end was a door flanked by a pair of arrow-straight Klingon guards. Kor used an electronic key attuned to the electron levels of the lock alloy to open the door. They entered, saw a small, dimly lit room. The room itself was almost empty and as warm as the outside. Some stands holding a smattering of scientific equipment were placed around the chamber. Cases and cabinetry lined one wall. At the far end was a bench supporting a medium-sized glass case.

"In there, gentlemen," Kor advised them as he pointed toward the case, "lies the Pandronian Tam Paupa. If local records are accurate, and we have no reason to believe they lie, the most frantic search the Pandronians could mount would not locate another for at least two hundred of their years. Their government and civilization should collapse inside forty."

"I can see why it's so difficult to locate," McCoy commented, squinting. "I can't see it even now."

"The inferiority of the human form," smirked Kor.

"That may be," Spock conceded, drawing a vicious glare from McCoy, "but it does not apply to me, and I see nothing inside that case save some shredded vegetable matter."

Kor's smirk gave way slowly to confusion as he also stared at the case. "It should be in plain view," he muttered. "Watch them closely," he directed the guards as he walked rapidly toward the bench. He looked down into the case.

"Odd." Taking a metal probe, he reached inside and stirred the bark shavings which apparently served to cushion the Tam Paupa. His stirrings grew frantic.

"Something the matter, Kor?" Kirk wondered pleasantly. But the Klingon captain's eyes had widened and he showed no sign of having heard.

"Guard—chamber guards!" Both tall Klingons who flanked the doorway stuck their heads into the chamber.

"Has anyone had access to this chamber since," and he hurriedly checked his personal chronometer, "eight *fluas* ago?"

Looking puzzled, the guard replied in Klingon, "No, Honored Captain. But we assumed duty only six *fluas* ago."

"Get back to your post!" Kor screamed. Rushing to one of the cabinets lining the left-hand wall, he thumbed an intercom switch, then spoke in Klingon, which all three officers understood reasonably well.

"Security Central . . . this is Captain Kor speaking. Who was on duty in the secure chamber as of seven *fluas* back?" A pause, then, "And for the period before that?" Another pause, followed by a violent command: "Get all of them up here immediately! I don't care if they are on rest period!" Kor's voice dropped menacingly. "Would you like your head separated from its shoulders like a Pandronian? You'll find reattaching it not so simple."

They waited while Kor glared furiously from empty

case to intercom and kicked at another cabinet as if it were personally responsible for his troubles. Abruptly his attention returned as someone reported at the other end of the intercom.

"Yes—what is your name and rank? This is Captain Kor, that's who, you lower-grade moron! And stop trembling—it garbles your words. Now, think carefully, if you are capable of such: Who had access to the secure chamber where the alien Tam Paupa thing was being kept? Only him? You are certain? Very well . . . No, you are not to be disciplined. Return to your activity previous. It matters nothing now."

He clicked off, stared blankly at the floor.

"Well?" Kirk prompted, unable to keep silent. Kor did not look up immediately.

"I had wondered why eb Riss had not come along to enjoy this victory," the Klingon murmured with barely controlled fury. "It is now clear he was planning one of his own."

"Such loyalty does a Klingon inspire among its minions," McCoy whispered, soft enough so that Kor didn't hear. In any case, the captain had other matters on his mind as he activated the intercom once again.

"Stables? Yes, I suspected. Who could have guessed? Prepare the others for emergency run. Yes, immediately." A quick flip transferred him to a different department. "Security Central—this is Captain Kor. I want a full squad of our Pandronian allies and an Imperial platoon at the stables—yes, fully armed. I don't care what Headquarters will say if we have to use energy weapons—the Tam Paupa's been stolen. Yes, by Lud eb Riss, our"—he paused, then concluded, his voice dripping venom—"most trusted contact in the Pandronian government." He flipped off the intercom, faced a curious but not displeased triumvirate of Federation officers.

"The traitor has taken a *coryat,* which is capable of negotiating the swamps. There is only one way he could run, and that is through the pathway cleared by our experimental creatures. But we will catch him and

I will bring him back with me—alive, to know the exquisite refinements of Klingon justice."

Still under guard, they were led from the empty room. In passing, Kor gave an order to one of the chamber guards. "Get onto the intercom. I want all the captured Pandronians brought to the front entryway, even if interrogation has begun. I have no time to go to them in the holding pens."

"It shall be done, Honored One," the guard responded.

Moments later they were back at the entrance to the headquarters building, where they were soon joined by a troop of tired, worried-looking Pandronian soldiers led by Ari bn Bem. Pandronian rebels kept them packed tightly together.

Kor went straight to bn Bem. "I must know what Lud eb Riss is likely to do; therefore I must know what sort of person you consider him to be."

The commander looked uncertain, but replied offhandedly, "He is a traitor to his race; what more is there to know of him?"

"He has restolen the Tam Paupa," Kor explained, "and is even now riding for Tendrazin. What is he likely to do there?"

At this information a strange sort of verbal bubbling poured in increasing waves from bn Bem's mouth. Since the common soldiers could not understand Klingon, he translated Kor's announcement for them. Immediately they began to mimic his bubbling noises, some bubbling so hard they could barely keep their feet. Their heads and middle sections shifted on their bodies as if they were coming apart. Kirk recognized it from previous experience with bn Bem as the Pandronian equivalent of laughter.

Captain Kor was not amused. He drew a small sidearm from his waist. It was clearly not Pandronian in origin and differed also from the hand weapons held by the Pandronian rebels. It very much looked like a poorly disguised, standard-naval-issue Imperial energy weapon.

Kor pointed it at bn Bem's head. "I will burn you

integral by integral where you stand if such a disre-
spectful outburst occurs again. Tell *that* to your subordinates."

bn Bem dutifully translated and the laughter died
down. Despite the threat, the commander couldn't prevent himself from declaring, with some satisfaction,
"So have the traitors betrayed been. Is for justice too
perverted, but is pleasing still."

"You should choose your coconspirators with
greater care, Captain," Spock suggested, noticing the
Klingon's finger tightening on the trigger of his
weapon. Kor, properly distracted, stared back at
Spock. "We are now presented with an additional question of interest: To be precise, who here was using
whom?"

"Shut up, you," Kor ordered him warningly. Forget-
ting that he was about to kill bn Bem, he directed another question at the Pandronian. "What can we expect
eb Riss to try to do with the Tam Paupa?"

"To return it was clearly never of his intention," bn
Bem surmised. "By now should high council be incapable of acting with a Tam Paupa-less premier. eb Riss
intelligent is always, but now appears That One more
intelligent than any believed. Also cunning, also calcu-
lating.

"This One would guess Tendrazin That One will enter surreptitiously. Will move freely, as is his rank, in
government central. With aid of Tam Paupa, eb Riss
will have own abilities enhanced. This One believes he
could himself have anointed premier."

"The shortsighted imbecile," Kor rumbled. "Doesn't
he realize we can have him removed the same way we
removed the Tam Paupa from that doddering old fool
who is the present head of government?"

"That may not be as easy as it was the first time,"
Spock felt compelled to point out, moved by the logic
of it. "The present premier and his supporters had no
idea there were Klingons scheming on his world,
whereas eb Riss knows precisely where you're located
and what you're up to. He used you all along."

"To make himself supreme ruler of Pandro," Kirk

continued when Spock had finished. "If his plan succeeds and he makes himself premier, and if this brain-boosting Tam Paupa is all its cracked up to be, then I don't see how you can give him much trouble. This rebellion you're supporting will fail and you'll have to renegotiate your position on Pandro—this time bidding against the Federation. I know eb Riss's type—he'll be interested in joining up with the side that offers *him* the most, not the one that promises the best for Pandro."

"There'll be no such trouble if we catch him first," Kor reminded them sharply. His weapon came around to point at Kirk. "In any event, you three will not be around to witness the eventual outcome. I see no reason for putting off your demise any longer.

"You will be fed to one of the experiments. I could burn you here, but I dislike waste and inefficiency. Your partially consumed bodies will be rescued and at least one communicator activated. We will lower our screens long enough for your ship to locate your communicator signal and beam up your remains. They will accept the evidence of the marks on your corpses, and there will be none to dispute this." He gestured meaningfully with the weapon. "Outside, please."

Devoid of expression, the three men and the Pandronians were marched toward the exit. The guards at the wide doorway moved aside smartly and the transparent panels slid apart to let them pass.

Kirk had barely taken a step outside when a tremendous explosion slammed him hard to the ground. As he was trying to recover from the initial shock of the concussion, a second explosion occurred. Glass and metal fragments whistled over his head, followed instantly by a series of nonstop, slightly smaller eruptions.

"Spock, Bones—run for the rafts!"

They were on their feet then, nearly falling several times as continuous blasts shook the earth all around them, though the actual explosions came from behind. Kirk looked around, almost falling again, and saw bn Bem and the rest of the Pandronian soldiers following. In the confusion which had thrown everyone to the ground the well-trained Pandronian troops had reacted more professionally than the Klingon-led rebels. They had overpowered their guards at the cost of several casualties.

Now only Captain Kor and two Klingon guards remained outside, for the initial explosion had collapsed the entryway into the main building. Seeing that he was outmanned and now outgunned, Kor had time to visit a look of helpless rage on Kirk. It turned to panic when another eruption ripped the air behind them.

"The power station!" Kirk could hear him yell desperately. "Get to the backups quickly or everything is lost!"

An ear-splitting moaning sounded from behind and to the right as they ran. Kirk saw that a second abomination had come up alongside the first. Even as he watched, both horrors suddenly slipped five meters closer to the Klingon installation.

"What the hell's going on?!" McCoy shouted. His answer came from the scurrying blue bi-ped now running on his left.

"Told all This One that Lud eb Riss's cunning was great," bn Bem told him breathlessly as they raced into the jungle again. "Expected the traitor some pursuit from Klingons. Would guess he left charges to create confusion and panic among them."

"I heard Kor yell something about a power station," Kirk told the others, gasping for breath as they hurried along. The rafts should be close now.

"That would cause panic indeed, Captain," Spock concurred with enviable ease as he strode along nearby. "It means that the double-force barrier the Klingons have erected will come down, and that the central frequency-modulator installation will also be inoperative. It follows that the results of the Klingon biological experiments will soon be free of all restraints."

"Talk about Frankenstein unbound," McCoy panted.

"Frankenstein unbound? What is that?" Commander bn Bem wanted to know.

"I'll explain later," McCoy replied, "but basically it's

a Terran catch phrase meaning you'd better run like mad!"

Trees rose all around them now. Kirk stole a last glimpse backward. Energy bolts were beginning to rise from the smoking rubble that had been the Klingon station. Kirk couldn't see what they were firing at.

But he had a brief sight of one target as they reached the rafts. It raised three legs and four tentacles, each as big around as a shuttlecraft, and brought them down on the exterior of the main building they had been so briefly imprisoned in.

It was not an educated assault, but it was effective. The structure simply disappeared beneath thousands of kilograms of sheer mass. Screams began to sound above the noise of battle.

Every so often a Klingon energy beam would strike one of the several colossuses now assaulting the installation and burn a hole in it. A section or two of the creature would fall away, blackened and burning, without slowing its former body in the least.

"The Klingons are becoming victims of their own experiment," he noted aloud. "Poetic Justice."

"The justice will be more than poetic, Captain," Spock reminded him, "if eb Riss also had the foresight to destroy our rafts as he retreated."

But when they broke through the last thick brush above the narrow beach and tumbled gratefully to the water's edge, the two unsightly craft were exactly where they had been left, grounded on the gentle slope. To Kirk they were as beautiful as a Federation destroyer.

"It may be, Captain, that eb Riss was unable to move the heavy craft by himself, or he may not have wished to delay himself by doing so," Spock theorized, even as he was lending his own muscle to that of four Pandronians as they fought to slide one raft into the swamp sludge.

"Or he could have expected us to be trapped in the explosions," McCoy countered. "Captain Kor couldn't have chosen a better time to feed us to his pets."

Both rafts slid buoyantly into the murk. No group of

professional oarsmen could have moved those two
clumsy constructions faster through the water than did
the three men and squadron of bedraggled Pandronian
troops.

"Look!" McCoy shouted, pointing behind them.
They had already put some distance between themselves and the island.

Kirk turned, saw an enormous elephantine neck
stretched perhaps a hundred and fifty meters into the
sky. It towered far above the tallest of the island trees.

Six mouths formed the terminus, each filled with
teeth the size of concrete pillars. Two of the jaws were
crunching sections of metal wall, while another was devouring a thick cylindrical shape, munching on the
hard formed metal as though it were a cracker.

An eye-searing flash ensued, followed by a rolling
explosion. The momentary flare lit the swamp around
them and threw everyone on the rafts into eerie
shadow.

"That was a fuel tank, chemical type," Kirk finally
declared assuredly as he looked back.

The huge waving neck was swaying wildly about. All
six mouths and the gargoylish head they had been
mounted in were gone, as was about twenty meters of
upper neck. But the blackened, charred stump continued to flail about without ceasing.

"The danger now imminent is," bn Bem brooded as
he regarded the now distant horror. "All will proceed to
act as would any meat-eater. All must now obtain own
enormous masses of food to survive.

"*Varboxites* will flee in all directions from them,"
the commander explained. "Creatures' senses will
direct massive forms to largest mass in region which
flees not."

"What would that be?" Spock asked, already more
than suspecting the answer. bn Bem gazed at each of
them in turn before replying.

"In Tendrazin city, is naturally."

"I wonder if eb Riss foresaw that also," Kirk muttered. "Can they get through the swamp?"

"Are you kidding, Jim?" McCoy looked back toward

the island, which was now long since out of sight. "It would take nothing short of a thermonuclear demolition charge or a ship's phaser banks to slow any one of those babies."

"Mr. Spock?" Kirk inquired. Spock already had his communicator out, but shook his head after several tries.

"The interference shield generated by the Klingons has vanished, Captain, but there is still no indication we are being received by the *Enterprise*."

That meant that the damage inflicted by the Pandronian boarders still hadn't been repaired, Kirk reflected. They were on their own, then.

"Is hard to believe eb Riss would plan so well and not see results of destroying Klingon aliens' control machines," bn Bem was musing. "Must That One have some plan for turning creatures from Tendrazin."

"You still don't seem to grasp the magnitude of what eb Riss has done, Commander," Kirk advised him. "Turning on his own people, then turning on those who helped him— I wouldn't put it past him to sit idly by while the Klingons' monsters ravage the whole city. Then he could make himself supreme ruler of Pandro without worry of any interference whatsoever—not with the seat of government obliterated."

"This One cannot believe such crime even of such as eb Riss," a horrified bn Bem replied. And then he appeared to wilt slightly. "Still, has he participated in theft of Tam Paupa twice. Loyalty must remain only to self. Can This One sorrowfully put nothing past him. It may be that eb Riss is madder even than the rebels he once helped."

A shout sounded from the other raft. bn Bem looked attentive as he exchanged words with a particularly bedraggled Pandronian soldier. Then Kirk recognized the other speaker. It was the head tracker, the Pandronian who had led them to the edge of the swamp.

At the moment, he was gesturing at a passing tree. "Broken small branches and missing leaves," bn Bem informed the curious men. "All signs of a *coryat* taking sustenance while on the run.

"Could be another creature have been made, but tracker thinks sure a *coryat*. Is good sign that eb Riss traveling same direction."

"Any chance of our overtaking him?" Kirk asked.

bn Bem looked sad. "*Coryat* built for speed, can outrun *zintar*. And travels much faster than raft."

There was one more surprise waiting for them when the rafts grounded on the mainland the following day. The *zintars* were arranged in a circle, their three handlers camped behind the protective bulks and armed with dart sidearms.

bn Bem conversed with their own handler, ab Af, and learned that eb Riss had indeed been by this way. He had tried to surprise the group, but the handlers detected him too soon and he passed them by, presumably on his way to Tendrazin.

"eb Riss decided not to challenge three handlers and trained *zintars*," bn Bem concluded.

"Why should he risk himself?" McCoy declared. "He got what he really wanted—the Tam Paupa. The Klingons won't give him any trouble; they'll be lucky if any of them get off that island alive. And he knews no one can beat him to the capital."

"Can but try," bn Bem countered grimly. "We ride, gentlemen."

The situation was explained to the *zintar* handlers as the great tame animals were being mounted. Soon they were traveling at a startling pace back toward Tendrazin.

Somewhere within that huge old city, man and Pandronian alike knew, Pandro's greatest traitor in its civilized history had by now secreted himself.

X

Halfway back to the city Kirk nearly fell from his saddle in his haste to acknowledge the suddenly beeping communicator at his waist. The steady jounce of a *zintar* at the gallop nearly caused him to drop it under thundering feet—but he held on.

"Mine is also signaling, Captain," Spock reported.

"And mine, Jim!" added an excited McCoy.

Kirk took a deep breath, flipped the cover back, and spoke hesitantly into the pickup. "This is the captain speaking."

"Lieutenant Uhura still acting in command, sir. Mr. Scott remains partially incapacitated by the Pandronian low-grade stun beam. The effects have almost worn off, though. Nurse Chapel is confident there will be no permanent aftereffects."

"And the Pandronian boarders?" Kirk wondered.

"They succeeded in completely disabling our communications, Captain," she informed them as Kirk ducked a low-hanging vine. "Somehow they knew exactly where to go and how to get there. I don't understand. I thought the Pandronians weren't that advanced."

"They've had plenty of the wrong kind of help, Lieutenant," Kirk told her. "There are Klingons operating on Pandro—or, there were."

"Klingons!" A moment's silence, then, "But I thought the Pandronians hadn't decided—"

"They haven't, Lieutenant. This installation was present without either the approval or knowledge of the duly constituted Pandronian government. I'll explain later. For now, suffice to say that the Klingons had some typical Klingon ideas about exploiting the peculiar Pandronian ecology for their own uses. But we don't have to worry about them any more," he finished grimly. "Though you might keep a sharp watch for Klingon warships. Their base here had to be supplied periodically from outside."

"The ecology they played with is now running wild. According to Commander bn Bem, natural instinct will probably lead the animals involved to move toward the largest stable concentration of life on this part of the planet, which would be the Pandronian capital city. Now, what about other damage and casualties?"

"Several other paralyzed security personnel are also

showing signs of recovery, Captain," Uhura reported crisply. "Ship damage appears to have been limited to our communications facilities. Under Mr. Scott's supervision, though, we have manged to rig a ship-to-surface link sufficient to get in touch with you—though Mr. Scott insists he can't guarantee how long it will last. Do you want us to beam you up, Captain?"

Kirk was considering a reply when Uhura broke in again. "Captain, Mr. Sulu has sensor contact with another vessel." A long, tense pause while they waited helplessly for further information.

"What's happening up there, Uhura?" Kirk finally called, unable to stand the silence.

"I was awaiting identification, Captain," came the reply. "Klingon cruiser escorting a cargo ship. We can't beam them and they're not beaming us."

"Probably surprised to see you," Kirk ventured. "Their captain's undoubtedly wondering at the lack of response from the surface, not to mention the presence of the *Enterprise*. I suspect he'll remain silent in orbit, hoping we'll leave—which we will, eventually. But keep a close watch on them, and report any indication of impending hostilities, Lieutenant."

This was all he needed—a Klinglon cruiser confronting the *Enterprise* at this crucial moment. He had to decide—did they beam up to join the ship, or remain to try to help the Pandronians?

The Klingons were obviously here to supply their ruined base. When a party from the cruiser finally beamed down into the wreckage, Kirk was willing to bet the cruiser captain would head for home with a report, rather than chance a pitched battle with a Federation ship for no particular reason. But he couldn't be certain—not until the Klingon left orbit.

But while it remained, the *Enterprise* couldn't use its ship's weaponry to halt the attack on Tendrazin. That would put her in an untenable tactical position which would be like waving a red flag in front of the Klingon cruiser. No, they would have to try something else to halt the lumbering assault on the city, at least until the standoff above was broken somehow.

"What do you think, Spock, Bones? Should we beam up?"

Spock shook his head once, quickly, and McCoy grumbled without looking at Kirk, "The least we can do is try to fix the mess the Klingons have made of Pandro."

"Stand by in the Transporter Room, Lieutenant," Kirk announced into his communicator, "but we're not ready to beam up just yet. We've got something we have to do here first. We'll keep you advised."

Ahead, Commander Ari bn Bem executed the Pandronian equivalent of a smile.

"What about the Pandronians who boarded the ship?" Kirk asked.

"We're holding them in the security section of Sick Bay, Captain," came the reply from above. "No matter how small they can subdivide, I don't think they can slip through a force screen. They refuse to discuss their mission, but they admit to being part of some kind of fanatical Pandronian society."

"Fanatical doesn't half say it, Lieutenant," Kirk told her. "Keep them locked up, and whatever you do, don't let one of them get behind anybody."

"No chance of that now, sir," she assured him. "I only wish we'd known their true capabilities when they first beamed aboard."

"This seems to be the day to learn all about Pandronian capabilities," was Kirk's response. "The Klingons learned the hard way. Kirk out."

"*Enterprise* out."

Once they entered the government stables, bn Bem was first off a *zintar*. He waited impatiently for Kirk and the others to dismount.

"We must hurry to the government chambers and convey our information to the premier and the council. Action must in effect be put to wrest the Tam Paupa from the traitor eb Riss."

Alternately walking and running, they followed the commander through the winding corridors of the government building. A queried courier told them that the premier was presently meeting in session with the full high council of both Tendrazin city and planet Pandro.

"Are all in private meeting chamber," the dazed courier called as the commander and his three aliens rushed by her.

bn Bem led them upward. Eventually they confronted a high portal guarded by four armed Pandronians in purple and puce uniforms.

The officer in charge barred their way. "No one to be admitted is," he said resolutely. "High Council and premier in special meeting are."

"I am a high commander myself and envoy extraordinary to United Federation of Planets," bn Bem announced with dignity. "Has This One information vital to safety of city Tendrazin and all planet Pandro."

"Nevertheless," the officer replied, "This One's orders say clearly that we are to—"

"This One claims extraordinary over ordinary," bn Bem shot back, "on all integrals mine and rank of high commander."

"Overranked and absolved is This One," the guard admitted, executing a half bow. "Be it on your association, I admit you." He moved aside, directing the other guards to do likewise.

The door was shoved inward and bn Bem strode importantly into the chamber with the Federation contingent close behind.

Most of the room was taken up by a huge table in the form of an eight-pointed star. High-ranking Pandronians of varying age and venerability were seated at seven of the points. At the star-point farthest from the doorway sat the premier, who abruptly rose and stared at them in shock.

"You," the new premier of Pandro exclaimed, the Tam Paupa positioned securely on his head, "how did you escape from—?"

Lud eb Riss suddenly grew aware he was on the verge of saying too much. Slowly he assumed his seat again and left the startled gaping to the rest of the representatives in the chamber. Those exhalted Pandronians were no less stunned than the new arrivals. bn

Bem's hastily composed speech and declaration of emergency was totally forgotten.

"Lud eb Riss," he was finally able to stammer, "This One under arrest declares you as traitor to all Pandro intelligences!" Turning, the commander called back through the still-open door. "Officer of the guard." The officer who had first prevented them from entering came into the chamber, followed by two of his subordinates.

bn Bem pointed across the table. "Arrest Lud eb Riss, the usurper."

"Remain at your posts," eb Riss countered in a new, strangely commanding tone.

"Note the altered voice, Captain," Spock whispered to Kirk. "One of the benefits of wearing the Tam Paupa, apparently. It magnifies more than the decision-making ability of whoever wears it. eb Riss is clearly more than he was. It is no wonder the Pandronians have placed such faith in whoever the Tam Paupa was on."

The officer of the guard hesitated, took a step backward. eb Riss appeared satisfied and to be gaining confidence with every moment.

"What have you done, eb Riss," Kirk demanded to know, "with the real premier, Kau afdel Kaun?"

It wasn't eb Riss but one of the councilors seated at the table who supplied an answer. "Have you heard not? Old afdel Kaun died from the effort of trying to handle the affairs of his office without the aid of the Tam Paupa. The strain was for him too much. The final dissolution his body met these two days past." He gestured toward the far corner of the table.

"Is now Lud eb Riss, wearer of Tam Paupa, premier designate of planet Pandro, to be confirmed this day itself."

"But you can't make him your new premier!" an outraged McCoy insisted. "He's the one who's responsible for the theft of the Tam Paupa in the first place."

Expressions and reactions differed markedly from human ones, but there was no mistaking the shock that McCoy's startling accusation caused at the table.

Slowly, the attention of every councilor shifted to the premier's chair.

eb Riss appeared only momentarily shaken by the direct charge, but with the assistance of the Tam Paupa he quickly recovered his confidence—as would be demanded of any planetary leader in such a situation. Kirk had already realized they were not arguing against a single Pandronian, but a Pandronian plus one.

"This a monstrous lie is," eb Riss declaimed with certitude. "Has This One only just risked life and integration to return and warn of danger to city of Tendrazin from beasts created by alien enemy Klingons?"

It had to be the Tam Paupa's assistance again, Kirk realized in frustration, which had induced in eb Riss the brilliant ploy of both denying McCoy's charge and stealing their chance to warn the council of the impending threat at the same time.

"Lies, lies, more and greater lies!" a near-violent bn Bem objected, waving his arms so hard that his middle torso occasionally hopped clear off his hips. "Not only a usurper and blasphemer is eb Riss, but was he himself who cooperated with Klingon aliens and them enabled to produce their monsters on Pandro."

"See how at moment of most crucial need for confidence and stability they dissension and disruption attempt to sow," boomed eb Riss with sly power. "Commander bn Bem has by his stay with Federation aliens been corrupted. Must he for his own good be imprisoned.

"As for alien life forms, they no better than Klingons are. Only different in shapes and colors. They too wish use of Pandro for their own unknowable ends. Must they be executed immediately, to prevent false panicking of Tendrazin population with their wild, detrimental stories."

"This One—This One knows not what to do, which ones to believe," stuttered Dav pn Hon, the most experienced and respected of all the high councillors. "Wears eb Riss the true Tam Paupa, which knowledge and forthrightness guarantees. Says eb Riss one thing."

His gaze swung speculatively to the angry group of aliens fronted by the honorable Commander bn Bem.

"Produces Commander Ari bn Bem outworld aliens for confirmation of most grave charges. Says bn Bem one thing." He performed a Pandronian gesture indicative of utter uncertainty. "Who is This One, who is council to believe?"

Murmurs of agreement and similar confusion were heard around the polished table.

eb Riss addressed the wavering silence. "Believe in which person you must," he told them, "but whatever you believe, cannot you deny the true Tam Paupa." When this didn't produce an outburst of acclaim, eb Riss played his trump card.

"Anyways, is any present who can offer means of stopping creatures both sides say soon will Tendrazin be attacking?"

More worried mutterings from the assembled councillors. Now their attention shifted from one another to the four figures standing before the doorway.

bn Bem turned to the Federation officers. "Well, Kirk Captain," he asked hopefully, "can you help us?"

"I don't know," Kirk admitted. "Just a moment." Activating his communicator, he turned away from the curious assembly and whispered into the pickup. "Kirk to *Enterprise*."

"*Enterprise*," came the reply, toned to softness by Kirk's adjustment of the volume. "Uhura here, Captain."

"Is the you-know-what still you-know-where, Lieutenant?"

"It hasn't changed position, Captain," Uhura responded, matching Kirk's deliberate lack of specifics with some fast thinking of her own. There was a definite reason behind it. If eb Riss knew there was a Klingon cruiser standing off the planet, the situation could become twice as difficult as it already was.

"Thanks, Lieutenant. Kirk out."

"What about one of your dart-throwing mechanisms such as the *fasir*?" Spock inquired. "Would they not be effective against the Klingon creatures?"

"Perhaps, Spock Commander," bn Bem admitted. "But is not weapons a problem. Is hard for us to produce the dissolution drug. Is not nearly enough in supplies of Tendrazin, not in many cities, to stop creatures so big. Was not ever expected by us to have to fight such impossible accretions of integrals."

"You see," exclaimed eb Riss, taking quick advantage of his opponent's indecision, "they are against their own lies helpless, as well as against assault which soon will come against us. Whereas This One," he reminded them grandiosely, "who wears Tam Paupa is only one who can Tendrazin save. Only This One.

"But will This One save city," he warned them, meeting the eyes of every individual council member in turn, "only if am confirmed immediately and irrevocably by high council as new premier of planet Pandro." And he grinned a Pandronian grin, not at the thoughtful councillors but across the broad table at the anguished face of Commander Ari bn Bem.

"Must do something to stop the traitor, Kirk Captain," the commander pleaded. "Is nothing you can do?"

"Circumstances prevent us from using ship's weapons, Commander," Kirk told him sadly. "As for anything we could beam down, I just don't know. I don't have authorization to use heavy weapons on Pandro's surface, and I don't want to duplicate a Klingon treaty violation by doing so. Besides, I'm not sure a phaser cannon could stop those creatures, and transmitting enough ship's power to be effective would put a strain on the *Enterprise*'s systems which might prove fatal if certain other parties elect to make trouble. I just don't know." He turned to his first officer.

"I am truly sorry, Captain, but it appears we must make a choice whether or not to use modern energy weapons, whether to risk weakening the *Enterprise* or saving Tendrazin."

"What about duplicating the frequency used by the Klingons in their controller?" Kirk wanted to know.

Spock quashed that possibility instantly. "Highly unlikely, Captain. We would have to achieve in a few hours what Klingon scientists clearly took a considerable period to accomplish. We have no idea what the frequency in question was. To locate it requires more time than we have, by a substantial margin.

"Of course, we could have an extraordinary stroke of good luck and hit upon the precise frequency right off, but I consider that a possibility too distant to be worth considering. We must come up with a different methodology."

Kirk looked over at McCoy, who was apparently deep in thought. "You working on an idea, Bones?"

"I was just thinking, Jim. The Pandronians, according to Commander bn Bem, might be able to handle this attack with their own weapons. All they need is a sufficient supply of the dissolution drug. Well, I've been producing drugs in large quantity all my life. I don't see why the *Enterprise*'s organic synthesizers couldn't turn out all the drug the Pandronians need.

"Even so," he added cautiously, "I'm not sure massive doses of the Pandronian drug will be enough to reduce to harmlessness what's coming this way. The commander's right when he says it will take one helluva lot of the stuff poured into those hulks. They might still be big and strong enough by the time they reach the city to cause a lot of damage."

"Is true," bn Bem agreed woefully. "Even best efforts with drug could not reduce last two creatures we saw while leaving *varbox*."

"There's got to be a way to make it work," Kirk insisted, trying to will a solution into being. "There's *got* to be!"

"For yourselves see," eb Riss cried in triumph, "admit the aliens their helplessness to save city. Cannot they preserve you. Only can This One. For This One wears the Tam Paupa!"

"It just doesn't look possible, Jim," McCoy insisted. "Whichever way the Pandronians turn they're faced with a dog-eat-dog situation."

"Bones, if we risk transmitting ship's power and you-know-who decides to attack, then we . . . we . . ."

He paused. Enlightenment dawned on his face.

Spock's eyebrows went up slightly. "Whatever your immediate thought, Captain, I do not see how Terran canines can be involved in our present situation in any way."

"It's not that, Spock, it's—" Kirk started to explain, but the same thought apparently struck McCoy.

"It just might work, Jim."

The first officers eyebrows advanced to his hairline. "Terran canines *are* involved? Captain, I don't understand what—"

"It's just an expression, Spock," Kirk told him offhandedly, his attention on McCoy. "You're sure you can synthesize the dissolution drug the Pandronians use, Bones?"

"Unless its a much more complex protein chain than I suspect, I don't see any reason why not."

"And in sufficient quantities?"

McCoy nodded. "As much as is needed."

"Captain, may I point out again the size and flexibility of the creatures the Klingons produced."

"I'm not thinking of destroying them before they reach the city, Mr. Spock. It seems clear we haven't that capability. What I *am* thinking of is moving them to the point of least resistance."

"If you are thinking, Captain," the first officer declared, "of changing the path of these creatures the way we did the dranzer stampede on Ribal Two, I don't believe it will work. The situation here is not analogous. We are dealing with only a few colossal creatures instead of millions of smaller ones.

"Furthermore, there is no species link between our attackers as there was on Ribal. Each one is different from the next, and there exists nothing like a chosen leader."

"I'm not talking about trying to run them in a circle like we did on Ribal, Spock. Obviously, if what Captain Kor told us about their protein requirements is true, nothing could possibly turn them from the nearest large, stable source of meat, which is Tendrazin.

"But if we can mount enough dart launchers on either side of their approach path and keep a steady quantity of the drug raining into them, we should at least be able to force the two creatures on the flanks to move away from the source of irritation. In other words, they'll continue to advance, but packed closer and closer together. Then if we can shove them tight enough, the combination of pressure, threat, and the presence of so much protein so close should unnerve them enough to start attacking *each other*."

"I wish I had your confidence, Jim," McCoy told him, "but I must admit your idea has a chance."

Kirk looked for confirmation from his science chief. "Well, Mr. Spock?"

"On the surface it seems plausible, Captain," Spock admitted. "Yet," and he was straining to gather in a fleeting thought, "something about the very concept troubles me, and I cannot say precisely why."

"Have you any better suggestions?" Kirk asked hopefully.

"No, Captain, I do not. And my worry is not grounded in fact. The idea *seems* reasonable."

"A fool's plan," snorted the transmogrified eb Riss. "Can never work. Only This One can save you all. Must make your decision now."

"Just a minute!" Kirk shouted as several council members seemed about to speak. "You don't have to make your final decision yet. eb Riss is a traitor of hardly believable proportions."

"So say you," injected a solemn Dav pn Hon.

"But what if we're telling the truth?" Kirk argued anxiously. "Give our idea a chance. If we fail, and eb Riss is truly as omnipotent now as he'd like you to believe, then he can still save you."

Trapped by his own vanity, eb Riss was forced not to refute Kirk's appraisal of his self-proclaimed abilities.

"Dr. McCoy, Mr. Spock, and I think we can force these monsters to turn on themselves," Kirk went on determinedly. "If we fail in this, you can always turn to whatever miracle eb Riss has planned. But you must give us this chance! Afterwards, when the threat to Tendrazin has been eliminated, you can consider the question of who should be your next premier without having to do so under pressure. Isn't that worth striving for?"

Rumbles of uncertainty from the assembled councillors, ending in grudging assent.

"And as long as we're on the subject of saving Tendrazin," Kirk shot across at eb Riss, "I'd like to know just what your plan for saving the city is, anyway."

eb Riss sat up straight in his seat and folded his arms. On his head the Tam Paupa, a metallic green circle surrounded by decorative projections and sparkling cabochons, shone bright in the light from overhead.

"Surely, Kirk Captain, you cannot think This One will reveal idea for use until is confirmed as premier? This One will wait as need be until high council comes to realization of truth."

"Yeah," snapped McCoy, "even if that turns out to be too late to save Tendrazin."

eb Riss made a Pandronian shrug. "Has This One presented offer to council."

"Look," McCoy muttered, "why doesn't someone just walk up to him and yank that holy crown whatsis off his rotten head?"

"Is against all Pandronian law and histories," Dav pn Hon informed them. "Would any to take Tam Paupa from who is wearing it, That One would be as guilty as whoever first stole it."

"And never mind that the one who stole it is now wearing it," a frustrated Kirk muttered. "Try to get around *that* one." He glared at eb Riss. "Your treachery is worse than a Klingon's, eb Riss. I believe you'd sacrifice the entire capital city to further your own personal ambition. Human history has had its share of types like you."

"This One not threatened by alien comparisons," eb Riss declared with dignity. "This One has passed point where personal wishes matter. Must do what must do, and means this insisting on my terms. Tendrazin not in This One's hands now." He eyed Kirk challengingly. "In your hands, Kirk Captain."

"Have we no choice," another councillor lamented. He faced Kirk. "If you fail, Kirk Captain, we must turn to eb Riss, traitor though maybe he be, in hope of salvation. This is our way."

"I understand, sir," Kirk replied soberly. He activated his communicator. "Kirk to *Enterprise* ... Transporter Room."

"Transporter Room on standby—Ensign M'degu on station, sir."

"We're ready to beam aboard, Ensign. We—" He paused as a hand came down on his shoulder.

bn Bem looked hard at him. "This One would go with you, Kirk Captain." The commander was fighting to control his emotions. "To be of assistance to McCoy Doctor." He indicated his own waist band and its pouches. "Have in sidearm and weapon case several doses of dissolution drug. Will need to duplicate." He looked to his left.

"Is sufficient, McCoy Doctor?" he inquired, flipping open the case to show the half dozen darts within.

McCoy glanced at them, nodded. "Is sufficient, bn Bem Commander." He smiled broadly. Like Kirk's and Spock's, McCoy's opinion of the commander had come a long way since the latter had first set foot on the *Enterprise.*

"Besides," bn Bem added, glaring back across the table, "if remain here knowing what This One knows, may do something fatal to self and other party. Would be dangerous to leave This One behind. Might violently disassemble eb Riss, even though fight could end with Tam Paupa damaged."

"I see your point," Kirk said knowingly. His voice was directed to the communicator again. "Ensign, there will be four in the beam-up party. Mr. Spock, Dr. McCoy, myself, and Commander bn Bem. We're localized," he added as all four moved close together, "so don't worry about catching someone else. The transporter is holding the commander's pattern."

"I have it, sir," the transporter operator reported. "Stand by."

As the high council watched silently, the four figures

were engulfed in a storm of dissolution no Pandronian life form could match. Then they were gone, leaving the councillors to stare at one another—and with mixed emotions at the calm, assured form of the mentally inspired Lud eb Riss.

Once back on board ship, McCoy wasted no time, but set to work immediately with several of the ship's chemists and Spock's assistance to synthesize the dissolution drug contained in bn Bem's dart-syringes. As expected—and hoped—the drug turned out to be a comparatively simple organic construction, which the *Enterprise*'s organic fabricator had no trouble reproducing.

With production underway, Kirk was able to devote some time to considering the Klingon threat. Actually, it was a threat only on the basis of past incidents, for the cruiser sat close by its companion cargo vessel and offered no contact. That was fine with Kirk. Now if the Klingons would only cooperate by staying put and letting their minds puzzle over what had happened to their secret ground installation, he might just have enough time to work everything out.

It was while he was dividing his thoughts between the enemy cruiser on the main viewscreen and the timetable Spock had worked out for the approach of the creatures to Tendrazin that bn Bem approached him, leaning over the command chair with an apologetic expression on his blue face. "Your pardon for disturbing thoughts, Kirk Captain."

"That's all right, Commander. I wasn't having any brainstorms anyway. What can I do for you?"

bn Bem, for the first time since Kirk had known him, seemed to be having difficulty finding the right words. Finally, he murmured, "Is Pandronian problem but seems insoluble by methods Pandronian."

"If you're still worried about what we'll do if the drugs fail to act as planned—" Kirk started to say, but the commander waved him off.

"Is not that. If McCoy Doctor can produce enough dissolution drug and if your plan succeeds, will still remain matter of traitor eb Riss having possession of Tam Paupa. He will not give it up voluntarily."

Kirk didn't understand. "But once we've disposed of the threat to Tendrazin created by the Klingons' experiments, then can't the council deal with eb Riss without fear?"

"You still not comprehend fully importance of Tam Paupa, Kirk Captain," bn Bem tried to explain. "Remind you that no Pandronian can take Tam Paupa by force from whoever wears it. Also, consider that Pandronian who wears Tam Paupa is best suited for making decisions on all Pandro."

"Are you saying," Kirk muttered in disbelief, "that is spite of what we've told them about what eb Riss has done, the high council could still possibly confirm him as premier?"

"This One really knows not," bn Bem confessed worriedly. "Never in memory has such a series of circumstances followed. So high councillors face unique situation.

"Is merely advising you that your help may further be required before certainty of planet Pandro's alliance with your Federation is. As you said, eb Riss if he survives will for himself strongest bargain drive."

"I guess we've been underestimating the spiritual importance of this Tam Paupa all along," Kirk mused, "while concerning ourselves only with its biological effects."

"There may be a way, Captain, to part the Tam Paupa from eb Riss." Kirk looked across to where Spock was regarding bn Bem thoughtfully.

"According to the commander," Kirk reminded his science officer, "Pandronian law forbids the removal by force of the Tam Paupa from whoever wears it."

"Is so," confirmed a forlorn bn Bem. "Removal and exchange must be voluntary."

"I realize that, Commander," Spock replied. "It is merely an idea I have, not a concrete proposal. Give it a little more time."

XI

Four days later McCoy and his research team had not only cracked the organic code of the Pandronian dissolution drug and successfully reproduced it, but they were now drawing it from the ship's organic fabricator in hundred-liter batches.

Each fresh tank of the drug, after being tested for dissolution toxicity, was beamed down to the surface of Pandro. There, under the disdainfully aloof gaze of eb Riss, Commander bn Bem was overseeing the distribution of the liquid. Tendrazin's government armories were turning out hypodermic darts at a furious rate. After being suitably charged with drug from the *Enterprise,* these thousands upon thousands of loaded syringes were placed in the concealed *fasirs* and other dart-firing weapons that had been placed on both sides of the approach to the city.

Facing the distant *varbox* and much closer forest, a broad cultivated plain and cleared area separated the former from the outer, ancient city wall. On either side of the plain facing the approach path to the city, the Pandronians had labored mightily to create two earthen dikes nearly twenty meters high. These formed a wide *V*-shape leading to the city gates, the point of the *V* actually being somewhere inside the city.

Everyone was preparing for the coming attack on the assumption that no quantity of the drug could cause the creatures to turn back. Naturally, the modest walls of the city would never stop a charge from even the smallest of the Klingons' experiments. But they would serve to channel the oncoming behemoths a little faster into smaller and smaller quarters. They were also excellent sites on which to mount the Pandronian dart-throwers.

When word was passed to the *Enterprise* via the communicator given to bn Bem that the onrushing monstrosities were about to break clear of the forest, Kirk, Spock, and McCoy beamed down to join the city's defenders.

Sensing the nearness of a really substantial quantity of raw protein, the creatures had apparently increased their speed. Kirk had hoped they would have several more days to produce even more of the dissolution drug, but the increased speed wasn't the real reason for the upsetting of the defenders' timetable.

"We have had scouts out monitoring the approach the past three days, Kirk Captain," bn Bem told them as they walked toward an unknown destination. "It appears the creatures do not sleep. Yet all integrals do sleep."

"I believe I can see how that is managed," Spock essayed. "The beasts are so enormous that while a portion of the integrals comprising each one engages in rest, there are enough remaining which perform similar functions to keep the body going at all times."

They had entered a semimodern Pandronian building near the outskirts of the city and been whisked by elevator to the top.

"Should from here have good view, Kirk Captain," bn Bem assured them as they walked out onto the roof of the structure. The commander's assessment turned out to be accurate.

From a position forty meters above the ground and close to the city wall, Kirk could see all the way to the distant forest. Tendrazin lay spread out behind and on both sides, a modern capital city which had retained the charm of its ancestry. One of the attractive, well-kept relics was the old city wall, which was presently lined with dart-armed Pandronian soldiers who would form the last line of defense against the onslaught of an ecology gone mad. Beyond them, only cultivated fields of stabilized associative plants moved in the slight, warm breeze of morning.

Farther off lay the cleared area that separated Tendrazin from the forest proper. Stretching off to either side were the two low earthen walls which the Pandronians had so painfully erected, working in round-the-clock shifts.

"What if the creatures, dumb as they are, choose to turn?" Kirk wondered at a sudden thought. "Suppose they decide to attack the gunners mounted on the walls instead of continuing on toward the city?"

"If Captain Kor's description of their appetites was accurate, Jim, I don't think that's likely." McCoy seemed confident. "They haven't the brains, I don't think, to guess where the irritation will be coming from, and the few soldiers on the ramparts don't represent a thousandth of the potential meal in Tendrazin. No, they'll keep advancing on the city, all right."

"Has already small-scale evacuation been started," one of the assembled councillors told Kirk. "From far side of Tendrazin. Is younglings and elderly only, as precaution. Always precaution. Should your idea not work and that of the wearer of Tam Paupa," and he indicated eb Riss, who was staring interestedly across the plain, toward the forest, "not work, hope we to still save most of population, even if city destroyed is."

"I hope that's what it remains," Kirk told him, "just a precaution."

"A rider comes!" someone called out. Everyone rushed to the edge of the bordered roof. A single *coryat* was rushing toward the city from the forest fringe, both legs of the tall running animal swallowing up the intervening distance with long, loping strides. A moment later the rider himself, panting for breath but otherwise composed, had joined them on the rooftop.

"Are near to emerging from forest," he gasped. "Have all impossible ones increased their speed as they near the city."

"They detect food in ample amounts," McCoy commented, finding the prospect of anyone here ending up in some Klingon experiment's belly discouraging.

"Is noted," Dav pn Hon told the rider. "Have you and all riders done well." The rider, dismissed, took his leave. pn Hon turned to face Kirk.

"Are all gunners ready. Have been given your instructions to fire on nearest creatures and continue fire as long as are able, Kirk Captain. Should last long, thanks to ample supplies of drug produced by McCoy Doctor."

"Not me," objected an embarrassed McCoy. "I had plenty of help in analyzing the drug, and the ship's organic fabrication engineers did the real work."

"Even now is too late, yet still you to these aliens listen," came a stinging accusal from eb Riss. "For chance last to save Tendrazin, throw outworlders and bn Bem into prison and to me alone listen."

As the point of no return approached, several of the councillors appeared to waver slightly. They looked to pn Hon as their spokesman. He turned to face bn Bem, said quietly, "What you say first will we try, as have promised."

eb Riss snorted and turned away from them all. If he held any concern for his own hide he didn't show it. Or, Kirk mused, he might have been trembling inside, only to be calmed by the soothing actions of the Tam Paupa.

"Here they come," McCoy announced.

Trees were smashed aside, large bushes and ferns crushed to pulp under their weight, as out of the forest barrier came a collection of six to twelve of the most bizarre living creatures anywhere in the galaxy. Hopping, stumbling, rolling, they lumbered forward, differing from one another only in size and shape.

All were undisciplined assemblages of the most impossible arrangements of teeth, nostrils, eyes, legs, and other body parts. Kirk had to correct his initial appraisal: They differed from one another in one more respect, besides size and shape.

There was the question of which was most hideous.

The largest of them was hunched forward slightly to right of center. It was so enormous Kirk couldn't see it all, at least not well enough to estimate its true dimensions. One of the councillors, in spite of having been told what to expect, cried aloud. Another found the sight so repulsive he covered his eyes and turned away.

bn Bem was peering into a pair of Pandronian magnifiers. Moving them from left to right, he was surveying the *fasir* positions.

"Our gunners firing steady now are," he informed them. "As yet no change visible on creatures' progress, Kirk Captain."

"Give the drug and the gunners time," McCoy urged. "Its going to take every drop of dissolution drug to have any kind of effect on those leviathans."

Confirming the doctor's words, the monstrosities continued their advance on the city. They were into the cropland now, and the councillor representing Tendrazin and its surrounding lands moaned steadily at the destruction.

Flopping and crawling, somehow moving their stupendous bulks over the ground, they ignored the steady hail of dart-syringes as they progressed. Behind them lay long dark streaks—gouges in the land dug by sheer mass.

At this range the rain of darts formed two clouds of silvery mist on the flanks of the advance. "Still no observable effect," bn Bem reported. Then a hint of excitement entered his voice. "No, wait. On the right is something happening."

Kirk had noted it, too, without the need of magnifiers. So had Spock and McCoy.

It was a little thing, an almost imperceptible shift in one creature's actions—but at least it was a beginning. The monster on the far left, nearest the embankment and guns on that side, had appeared to flinch, its whole hundred-meter-high body arcing to the inside.

Moving inward, it scraped hard against the abomination next to it. Several jaws and grasping limbs on each creature snapped and dug at each other, but the two creatures continued to move forward, though now jammed tight together.

"It's working!" McCoy exclaimed. "The one on the inside was forced inward by the darts, Jim. The drug cost it too much of itself." And he pointed to the affected sections of the creature, which lay like large limp rags in a retreating line back toward the forest.

"It's working," Kirk agreed tightly, "so far."

"There—on the side other!" one of the councillors shouted. Everyone's gaze swerved to the other side of the broad open plain. Sure enough, the beast nearest the irritating weapons there had swung inward, shoving the next creature in to one side, where it pushed up against still another monster.

Sounds of rising fury began to become audible from the approaching armada of integrals, but they continued to come on.

"They're still not fighting, Jim," McCoy complained. "They're jammed almost on top of one another, but they're not fighting among themselves."

"It still has time to work, Bones," Kirk responded. "It has to work."

Pandronian soldiers at the forest end of the dirt ramparts who had now been passed by the marching monstrosities were struggling to move their mobile weapons down the line. As a result, the barrage of darts grew more intense the closer the creatures came to the city. By now they were near enough so that the men and the Pandronians on the rooftop could discern individual features on each animal.

Never in his wildest nightmares as a child had Kirk envisioned anything so ghastly as any one of the oncoming gargantuas. Tendrazin was being assaulted by creatures a dying addict could not have imagined in his most frenzied moments.

Now they were packed so close to one another by the dissolution drug that there was no room left for the creatures inside to move any direction but straight ahead. Any brains contained by the monsters were lost in the task of simply running the huge collection of integrals.

Kirk watched in absolute fascination as the rain of darts continued to strike the outside of the two creatures nearest the narrowing battlements. As each dart injected its tiny portion of drug, a small portion of creature would slough away, to run, hop, scramble back toward the forest, all will to integrate lost. Those on the flanks had lost considerable mass by now, but the remaining majority of creatures in between were only weakly affected.

"Something's got to happen soon," McCoy said nervously. "There's hardly enough room for them to move without stepping on each other."

At first it seemed as if McCoy was wrong, that the abominations would continue their inexorable side-by-side march on the city. But soon a great tintinnabulation arose among the heaving mass of integrated flesh, a cacophony produced by the simultaneous activating of ten thousand mouths.

Coming to a slow, ponderous halt, one creature turned furiously on its neighbor, and it in turn on the next, and it on yet another, so that soon jaws and limbs were engaged in a frightful battle the likes of which no world had ever seen.

"That's done it!" McCoy exulted. "They're attacking one another. They're going to . . . to . . ." His voice faded, crushed by the enormity of what was taking place out on the innocent plain.

"Oh, my God," Kirk murmured.

Indeed, the results of the Klingon experiment had begun to turn on one another—but not in the way Kirk had predicted, and in a fashion none had foreseen.

No more limbs were torn, no flesh ripped from a fellow mountain of integrals, no teeth dug great sores in the body pressing so claustrophobically upon it.

"They're not fighting any more," Kirk whispered in disbelief. "They're integrating with *each other*."

Panic had fallen like a wave on the high council. "Sound full evacuation!" one was yelling repeatedly. "All to retreat! Is lost Tendrazin . . . Is lost Pandro . . .!"

Gunners continued desperately to pour their unceasing hail of darts on the flanks of the attackers, which were attackers no longer. In their place the ultimate horror had been created, forced for survival to close integral ranks instead of fighting among itself. Under the constant prodding of the dissolution drug, the lumbering horrors had blended, joined to form one single, awesome, pulsating mountain of flesh. It towered above the highest structures of central Tendrazin and cast a long, threatening shadow over the plain and city wall behind which Kirk and the others stood.

So enormous was it that it blocked out the sun. Thousands of jaws bellowed and snapped along its front and sides, thousands more eyes of all shapes, sizes, and colors rolled madly in all directions. With a heave that shook the ground, the Pandronian mountain threw itself forward in a half hop, half fall. The action was repeated again, covering more distance this time.

With energy born of desperation the gunners on the enbankments flanking the quivering hulk poured more and more of the dissolution drug into its clifflike sides. Integrals continued to fall and tumble from the creature's sides, looking like pebbles bouncing down a canyon wall.

"It's not going to work, Jim," a frantic McCoy declared. "We've failed."

"It's my fault, Bones," a disconsolate Kirk replied. "I didn't imagine this possibility."

"Do not blame yourself, Captain." Spock viewed the catastrophe with typical detachment. "Neither did I, though something was bothering me about the concept from the first. Who would dream that the attackers would combine to create one invulnerable beast instead of fighting one another, as would be expected of carnivores in such a situation."

"There's still one last chance, Spock."

The first officer noticed the wild gleam in Kirk's eye. "Captain, I must object. We cannot transmit ship's power. To so weaken the *Enterprise* while it lies in range of a potentially belligerent enemy vessel—"

"I know, Spock, I know!" Kirk's voice was agonized as he fought to make the decision, while the oncoming colossus rolled steadily nearer.

The Pandronians could not wait for Kirk to make up his mind. All had rushed as one to stand before eb Riss, who glared down at them, apparently indifferent to approaching annihilation. They took turns pleading with the wearer of the Tam Paupa to save them, as

Pandronians had done for thousands of years in moments of crisis.

eb Riss finally deigned to speak. "Is This One confirmed as premier?"

"Yes—yes!" several voices acknowledged hastily.

"Too easy," eb Riss objected. "It must by the Oath of dn Mida be so sworn."

The members of the high council began to recite in Pandronian a long, involved, unchallengable oath. When concluded, it would irrevocably install the traitor eb Riss as supreme head of the planetary government—no matter what anyone might decide subsequently. Having been sworn in by that oath, eb Riss could not be removed from office.

It looked, Kirk thought, as if the master Pandronian manipulator was about to gain everything he had planned from the very beginning. eb Riss had made use of Kirk and his companions, of the Klingons, and of his own people to achieve absolute power.

And there didn't appear to be any way to stop him.

"Hold your oath a moment. Councillors of Pandro!" Spock's cry was loud and strident enough to startle the councillors to silence.

eb Riss eyed Spock warningly. "Listen not to this alien outworlder. Finish the oath!"

Spock turned, pointed toward the field. "Closely to look at what happening is, gentlemen," he insisted in halting Pandronian.

In spite of themselves, in spite of the anxiety of the moment, all of the council members gave in to the urge to see what this strange alien was so insistent about.

"It—it's stopped," McCoy stammered in amazement.

Similar wondrous mutterings rose from the group of high councillors, for truly, the ontumbling mountain had come to a halt.

"The organism has reached a critical organic mass," Spock explained to the mermerized onlookers. "The demands of an impossible body have overridden the arguments of its nervous systems. Organic demands insist that it can proceed no further without massive ingestions of food. And food it will have."

All gaped as thousands of mouths tore at the flesh nearest to their respective maws, shredding limbs and scales, necks and motile limbs in a frenzy of hunger.

"It's devouring itself," Kirk said for all of them.

"One section no longer can communicate with another," the first officer went on. "Internal communication has collapsed under the all-consuming need for sustenance.

"It has become big enough to go mad."

Steadily one section of the monster vanished into another, all internal direction submerged in the orgy of mindless feeding. Soon the irrigated croplands just outside the old city wall were awash in a sea of Pandronian animal blood. Claws and fangs continued to rip away at helpless body parts.

The rejuvenated Pandronian gunners had no time to cheer. They were too busy, continuing to pour an unending flood of drug-laden darts into undamaged integrals. Now the individual sections of the creature commenced to fall away in clumps instead of single components. The retreat of disassociated integrals back toward the forest grew from a steady stream into a stampede.

Between its own depredations and the effects of the massive infusion of drug, the ultimate monster dissolved like a steak in an acid bath.

"Will they ever recombine?" Kirk mused.

"I think not, Captain," ventured Spock. "The effects of the dissolution drug are long-lasting. In any event, it was only the Klingon hormones and frequency controller that induced the component integrals to combine into such huge, unnatural associations. That hormone is now being broken down by the dissolution chemicals. Those integrals which are not drugged will likely experience no desire, retain no drive, to form anything other than natural integrations again."

By now the monster had shrunk to half its initial size. Dead sections, paralyzed or wounded integrals began to pile up around its pulsing base like so much living talus. At the rate dissolution was proceeding, the creature would shortly be reduced to manageable proportions. It already appeared to Kirk that the number of wounded or dying integrals exceeded the healthy ones still constituting the living body.

"We give thanks to you for aid," Commander bn Bem told Kirk gratefully, "for having Tendrazin saved from greater evil than could be imagined." Turning, he addressed the silent council members.

"Have done the outworlders of the Federation what they said could be done, what This One said they could do. Have we now another task before us of equal importance." His gaze went past them. "To choose new premier of planet Pandro."

Somehow a shaken eb Riss managed to retain a modicum of composure, although his previous arrogant confidence had vanished. If it weren't for the Tam Paupa he wore, Kirk suspected, eb Riss would long since have been running for the nearest exit.

"Still This One wears the Tam Paupa," he boomed shakily. "Are among you any who would oldest Pandronian law violate to take it from me?"

Not one of the by-now-angry councillors took a step forward, nor did bn Bem.

"What are we to do, Kirk Captain?" he wondered, bemoaning the seeming standoff. "Cannot anyone take Tam Paupa from wearer without incurring wrath of all Pandronians past. Cannot we confirm nonperson eb Riss as premier, but cannot we have premier without Tam Paupa."

"I still don't see why the situation doesn't warrant an exception to the law," Kirk objected. "For this one time, can't you try and— Spock?" He broke off, staring at his first officer, who was standing utterly motionless, looking into nothingness. "Spock, are you all right?"

McCoy had noticed Spock enter his present state from the beginning, and he cautioned Kirk, "Easy, Jim—Vulcan mind trance."

Already Kirk had noticed the familiarity of Spock's peculiar vacant expression. The Vulcan body swayed ever so slightly, but remained otherwise rigid. Kirk followed the direction of that blank gaze of concentration and discovered it was focused directly on Lud eb Riss.

Gradually that Pandronian's air of determined defiance faded, to be replaced quickly by first a look of uncertainty and then one of alarm. On his head the Tam Paupa seemed to quiver, just a hair.

"No," eb Riss stammered, stepping back away from Spock. "Stop now, Outworlder!"

But Spock's attitude did not change one iota, and the Tam Paupa's quivering increased. Kirk, McCoy, and the other Pandronians were united in their dumbfounded feeling—but for different reasons.

Kirk had no idea what Spock was up to, but he knew better than to try to question or interfere while his friend and second in command was locked in that trance.

The oscillation of the Tam Paupa continued to increase, until a fully panicked eb Riss was forced to put his hands to his head to try to steady it. Both hands came away as if the Pandronian had immersed them in fire.

Something else seemed to go out of the traitor. He stumbled backward blindly, crashed into the restraining wall lining the top of the building, and slumped to a sitting position. He wore the look of a badly beaten boxer.

At that point, when Kirk began to feel he was gaining some understanding of what was going on, something happened which dropped his lower jaw a full centimeter.

Rising on a ring of glistening cilia, the Tam Paupa lifted itself into the air. Microscopically fine filaments withdrew bloodlessly from a circle around eb Riss's scalp. As he stared in disbelief, Kirk could just barely make out a line of tiny eyes, much like those of a spider, running around the front rim of the brilliantly colored circle.

What had given the appearance of metal now revealed itself as organic, having the same sheen as a shiny-scaled Terran lizard. Gemlike bulges in front now declared themselves to be eyes, which stayed glazed over while the Tam Paupa was being worn.

While eb Riss lay like one paralyzed, the Tam Paupa slowly crawled off his head, down his face, and away from his body.

"I'll be an imploded star," Kirk exclaimed, "the blasted thing's alive!"

bn Bem spared a moment to turn a curious look on Kirk. "Of course is alive the Tam Paupa. You mean you knew this not?"

"We thought," murmured McCoy, "it was some kind of crown."

"Is crown truly. Is crown alive," the commander hastened to explain. "Why you think we not make new Tam Paupa when this one first stolen?"

"We thought this one had some particular cultural or spiritual significance," Kirk reasoned.

"Has that," admitted bn Bem, "but is much more why. Tam Paupa is maybe rarest integral on Pandro. One found only every two to five hundred our years. Is why this one missed so badly. Immature Tam Paupa types live plentiful, but useless to us. Have no ability to integrate with Pandronian mind, to aid in decision-making."

"It's an intelligent creature, then?" a skeptical McCoy wondered.

"Not intelligence as we say," the commander continued. "Is most specialized integral—perhaps most specialized on all planet Pandro." He frowned a Pandronian frown.

"But This One not understand why it left eb Riss. eb Riss not dead."

"What happens when the Pandronian wearing—no, I guess I should say associating—with the Tam Paupa does die?" McCoy inquired. "Surely Pandronians don't live six hundred years or so."

"No. When that happens, council or similar group of potential premiers is assembled. At moment of decision Tam Paupa leaves now useless body of former integration and chooses new one to associate with. That One becomes new ruler of Pandro.

"Is most fair and efficient method of choosing new Pandro leader. Tam Paupa always selects best mind present to associate self with. Is also why Pandro never have any fat premiers," the commander added as an afterthought. "Tam Paupa draws sustenance as uneating integral from its Pandronian host-partner."

"Sort of like a mental tapeworm," McCoy observed fascinatedly.

"But still remains question, why Tam Paupa leave eb Riss traitor? Is That One not dead," and he gestured at the dazed but still very much alive eb Riss.

"I think maybe I can answer that," Kirk said slowly. "When he enters a Vulcan mind trance, Mr. Spock is capable of mental communication to a certain degree. What he's doing to, or with, the Tam Paupa I can't imagine, but he's obviously doing *something*.

"I wonder how long Spock's known that the Tam Paupa was a living creature and not a hunk of metal, Bones."

"No telling, Jim," the doctor replied. "Could have been from the beginning, or he might have discovered it just now. We never discussed it among ourselves, so if he did know, he probably saw no reason to bring the subject up. Besides, you know Spock when he really gets interested in something."

"I know, Bones. Sometimes he forgets that the rest of us might not see things as clearly as he does," Kirk noted. "And speaking of seeing things clearly . . ." He pointed downward.

After a long pause next to eb Riss's motionless body, the Tam Paupa had apparently concluded its scrutiny of the assembled prospective candidates. It began to move again on its hundreds of tiny cilia—directly toward Spock.

"We've got to wake him up, Jim," McCoy exclaimed, alarmed at the direction events were taking. "He may not be aware of what's happening." Indeed, the *Enterprise*'s first officer was still staring off into space, and not down at the shining circle approaching his feet.

"Bones, I don't know. Maybe—" Kirk moved to intercept the creature, bending and reaching down with a hand.

A strong blue arm grabbed his shoulder, pulled him back. "No, Kirk Captain," bn Bem warned him. "Not to touch the Tam Paupa. Recall that creature which can live six hundred Pandronian years in unstable jungles of Pandro has defenses other than mental. Recall recent actions of traitor eb Riss."

Kirk thought back a moment. When eb Riss had sought to prevent the Tam Paupa from leaving him, he had reached up with his hands—and promptly yanked them away, in evident pain. Now Kirk scrutinized those limp hands and saw that they were burned almost beyond recognition.

"When so wishes, can Tam Paupa secrete extremely caustic substance for protection," bn Bem went on to explain. "Protects self also from disassociation, even while wearer sleeps."

"Then how the devil," McCoy wondered, "did the rebels manage to remove it from old afdel Kaun?"

"That answer's obvious, Bones, if you stop a minute and think."

"Sure—the Klingons have methods of handling anything, like we do, no matter how corrosive. They must have supplied the rebels who committed the actual theft with everything they needed." His attention was directed downward.

"Right now I'm more concerned with what that impressive little symbiote has on its mind," the doctor finished, voicing professional concern.

"We can't stop it, Bones," a tight-voiced Kirk reminded him, "and it would be highly dangerous to try beaming Spock up while he's still in trance state. He must have known what he was chancing when he began this. Let's hope he has some control over what's happening now."

The first officer of the *Enterprise* showed no sign of retreat or awakening, however, as the Tam Paupa continued its deliberate approach. Although Kirk knew it was a benign creature, he couldn't help comparing the scene to a large spider stalking its prey.

Reaching Spock's feet, the front end of the Tam Paupa touched his left boot. Kirk stiffened, started to reach for the hand phaser at his hip—no matter the consequences to Pandro if he vaporized the creature. More important were the consequences to Spock.

But his hand paused when the creature did. It remained there for long minutes, and Kirk wondered if it could detect his implied threat to kill. Abruptly, it backed away, hesitated again, and this time started straight for Commander Ari bn Bem.

With a mixture of excitement and horrid fascination, Kirk and McCoy stared as the creature touched bn Bem's foot, crawled up the back of his right leg, crossed his chest, went up the back of his neck, and settled itself like a bird scrunching down in its nest on the commander's head.

bn Bem's eyes had closed and remained closed when the Tam Paupa first touched him. Now they opened, and a different bn Bem looked out on the world. It was the look of a wiser Pandronian, one more compassionate and understanding, devoid of the omnipresent arrogance of Pandro.

"Is done," he told the councillors in a deep voice. "Has chosen the Tam Paupa." One by one he locked eyes with the assembled high council members. One by one they wordlessly confirmed him as premier. No oaths or formalities were required, not now.

"Have we been without a leader too long," declaimed High Councillor Dav pn Hon. "Commander former Ari bn Bem, are you now legitimate Premier Ari afbn Bem, ruler of planet Pandro. Done this moment by choice of high council and the true Tam Paupa."

"Is good this resolved well," afbn Bem agreed, without a hint of smugness or personal satisfaction in his voice at the Tam Paupa's choice. He turned now, to face the approving gazes of Kirk and McCoy—and of Spock, whose trance had broken the moment the Tam Paupa had settled itself on the commander's head.

"All thanks is to you, Kirk Captain, McCoy Doctor,

Spock Commander. Is once again government of Pandro stabilized."

But while Kirk heard every word the commander said, his attention was focused irresistibly on the Pandronian's forehead. Somewhere in a circular line there, he knew, thin silky filaments had been sunk through the skin into afbn Bem's head, probably into the brain itself.

Hard as he peered, he could see no hint of the connection, so fine were the filaments involved. His gaze moved slightly higher, to note that once more the multiple eyes had glazed over. Again they resembled so many jewels set in a motionless crown.

The Tam Paupa, content in its new partner, was at peace. So apparently, was Ari afbn Bem, and so was the government of Pandro.

"To you, Spock Commander," the new premier was saying, "must go highest of all thanks."

"It was the only way," a diffident science officer replied modestly. He was rubbing his temples. The strain of holding the mind trance was always somewhat wearying.

"What way, Spock?" asked McCoy. "How did you do it?"

"Naturally it was clear the Tam Paupa could not be forcibly taken from eb Riss," Spock went on to explain. "Not only would the Tam Paupa resist with its own particular defenses, but the shock of tearing loose the filaments would have killed it, as well as eb Riss. Only with advanced medical technology could it be done. That's what the Klingons obviously employed in removing it from afdel Kaun, but we had no time to engage in even modest surgery." McCoy nodded in agreement.

"I had gradually grown aware that the Tam Paupa was a living organism complete unto itself, and found myself drawn to study of its extraordinary circular brain."

"Circular brain?" Kirk muttered.

"Yes, Captain. Functions of both spinal cord and brain are combined in one organ which runs the entire circumference of the body.

"Only recently did I feel I might be able to contact that unique mind. We did not actually engage in mental speech or telepathy of any kind. It was more in the nature of exchanging whole concepts all at once.

"I concentrated on communicating one thing to it: that Lud eb Riss was an unsuitable host. The Tam Paupa was uncertain. I tried to show it that while eb Riss's mind might be organically sound, its decision-making process was aberrant and diseased. To illustrate this, I used examples of eb Riss's recent behavior in an attempt to convince the Tam Paupa that such a mind was not a healthy associative partner because it could at any moment turn upon itself.

"In other words, I tried to show that by logical standards—and the Tam Paupa is a very logical organism, Captain—eb Riss was insane. In the end, the creature agreed with me and left eb Riss for a more suitable partner." He indicated afbn Bem, who was standing nearby, listening with interest.

"Yet it started for you first, Spock," Kirk pointed out.

Spock looked mildly discomfited for a minute. "I had only conceived of persuading the creature to abandon eb Riss, Captain. I did not consider that once having done this it might settle upon me as the most reasonable new host. Had the creature persisted in its first decision I do not know what might have happened.

"Nor could I break the mental link I had so firmly established between it and myself. Had it completed a full integration with my mind, assuming it could do so with a non-Pandronian life form, I suspect I would have ended up resigning my commission and remaining here for the rest of my natural life as ruler of Pandro."

"*Spock!*" McCoy looked aghast.

"I had no choice in the matter, Doctor," the first officer insisted, turning to face him. "The Tam Paupa's power is concentrated foremost on its own needs. I could *not* break that mental bridge. For so small a creature its mental strength is quite incredible.

"Fortunately, it decided at the last minute, perhaps partially as a result of reading the reluctance in my mind, that my resistance to the prospect of ruling Pandro was so strong that it eliminated me as a suitable host. A more receptive mind was required, hopefully one which would actually welcome the prospect of ruling the planet. It chose, as we have seen, Commander bn Bem."

"Don't tell me the Tam Paupa has a compulsion to rule, Spock," McCoy commented in disbelief.

"No, Doctor, it is not that at all. But if you wished to maximize your opportunities for a good life, what better person to associate with than the supreme ruler of the dominant race of the world you live on? It is the Tam Paupa's way of optimizing its survival quotient."

"Argue we not with the Tam Paupa's choice," declared the elderly pn Hon. "Is known well to us Premier afbn Bem's integrity and abilities. Still," and he looked puzzled, "are many present with longer experience and, intending no impoliteness, greater administrative talents. Why, then, Ari bn Bem chosen?"

"I can hazard a guess," Spock told him.

Kirk nodded. "Go ahead and hazard, Mr. Spock."

"Remember our experience on Delta Theta Three, Captain. Commander bn Bem was exposed to the influence of the planetary mother-mind. As we subsequently observed, his attitude was altered significantly for the better by that chastising encounter.

"Perceptive a creature as the Tam Paupa is, I have no doubt that it detected this shift in normal Pandronian state of mind, which none of the other councillors present have had the benefit of."

"What about him?" McCoy demanded to know, compelled by professional concern to pay more attention than he desired to the only suffering member of the group.

"eb Riss?" a councillor said, noting the direction of McCoy's gaze. "We do not believe in killing, though never was it so warranted."

"We will not kill him outright," bn Bem explained, "but will he be given maximum punishment under Pandronian law. He will a massive dose of the dissolution formula be given, so that his integrals no longer one another will be able to stand. As all such criminals deserve, he will to wander the streets and fields of Pandro be condemned—in pieces, never again to exist as a fully-functioning Pandronian."

McCoy shivered. "I don't think I'd care to spend the rest of my life not knowing where my arms and legs and body were. No, I'd far rather be killed."

"Is not quite same sensation for Pandronian, McCoy Doctor," afbn Bem told him. "But will insure eb Riss harms no one ever again."

Under order from one of the concillors, guards were called and Lud eb Riss was led away to his fate.

"Owe we you all an immeasurable debt, Kirk Captain," the new premier declared when eb Riss had been removed. "Not only This One personally, but all planet Pandro. Is little enough, but can This One assure you that high council will soon approve application for associative member status in United Federation of Planets."

"That ought to make the Klingons happy," chuckled McCoy.

"Depart in harmony and full integration," afbn Bem told them. "To return as soon as are permitted, Kirk Captain. Will then see some changes made in Pandro and Pandronian attitudes, of which I was once worst example."

"I'm sure you'll make a fine premier, Commander," replied a gratified Kirk, "with the Tam Paupa to help you." He activated his communicator. "Kirk to *Enterprise*."

"*Enterprise*—Scott here—finally."

"Scotty!" exclaimed a surprised but pleased Kirk. "You're all right again."

"Aye, Captain," the chief engineer replied, obviously in high spirits. "The paralysis was temporary, as Nurse Chapel decided it would be. I'm fully recovered."

"And the other crew members who were affected?" McCoy inquired over his own communicator.

"They're all comin' along fine, Dr. McCoy. Chapel says they should all be up and about in a couple of days."

"All good news, Scotty," responded Kirk, "and just as good down here. You can beam the three of us up. We're finished. Pandro is going to join the Federation and our old friend Commander bn Bem has just been made premier."

"bn Bem?" Scott muttered uncertainly, unaware as he was of the commander's complete transformation. "Captain, are you certain . . .?"

"He's changed quite a bit since he first stepped on board the *Enterprise,* Scotty, and he's the first to admit that it's been for the better. Also, the Klingons have experienced a severe case of diplomatic foot-in-mouth disease."

"That doesn't send me into fits of depression, Captain."

"I didn't think it would, Scotty. Whenever you're ready."

"Aye, Captain. Stand by."

The entire Pandronian high council snapped to attention. Led by their new premier, every member performed an intricate Pandronian salute as Kirk, McCoy, and Spock dissolved in pillars of fire and vanished from the surface of Pandro.

As soon as he was sure transportation was proceeding normally, Scott left the conclusion of the operation to his assistant and rushed toward the alcove. He was moving to shake Kirk's hand almost before final recomposition was completed.

"Good to see you back on your feet, Scotty," was Kirk's first observation as he stepped down from the alcove.

"There don't seem to be any aftereffects, either, Captain," his chief engineer informed him. "I'd be willin' to bet that the Klingon's Pandronian allies were so unstable and unpredictable that they couldn't be trusted with really dangerous weapons."

"I'd come to the same conclusion, Scotty, even allowing for the demolition equipment they brought on board. They're still in custody?"

"Aye, Captain."

"You can direct Security to bring them here and

beam them down to the surface. Use our last coordinates. I think they'll find a suitable reception waiting for them."

"With pleasure," Scott replied. "A more sour and fanatical bunch I've never encountered. It's a good thing Uhura was the one who interviewed them. I dinna think I would have been quite so gentle."

Kirk nodded, turned to his companions. "Mr. Spock, Bones, we'd better be getting up to the bridge."

"If you don't mind, Jim," McCoy murmured, "I'd just as soon check on those injured security people first."

"Of course, Bones. I forgot." McCoy smiled slightly, left quickly for Sick Bay.

Although still on full alert because of the presence of the Klingon cruiser nearby, it was an understandably happy bridge crew that noted Kirk and Spock's reappearance. There were no shouts of joy, no demonstrations. But nothing in the regulations forbade personnel under alert status from smiling, and everyone seemed to straighten slightly.

"Any change in the Klingons' position, Mr. Sulu?"

"None, Captain," the helmsman replied. "They're still just sitting there."

"Our communications are functioning again, Captain," Uhura put in. "Should I try to contact them now?"

Kirk considered, then smiled a little himself. "No, Lieutenant. Never mind. They know we know they're here. They're probably waiting and hoping that we don't start anything, or just go away. We'll oblige them. Any sign of transporter activity since they arrived, Mr. Sulu?"

"No, sir."

Kirk appeared satisfied. "Naturally not. They're afraid we'd detect it and want to know what they were up to on a neutral world. They must be frantic with worry, since they haven't been able to raise their secret installation. I don't think they're going to like what they find.

"Mr. Arex, lay in a course for Starbase Sixteen.

Much as I'd like to be around when the Klingons discover what's happened on Pandro, I'd prefer to avoid unnecessary hostilities. And the Klingons are going to be feeling particularly hostile."

Navigator and helmsman moved to execute the order. As they were preparing to do so, Kirk noticed that his first officer seemed in an especially thoughtful mood.

"What is it, Spock?" Abruptly he had a thought of his own. "Don't tell me you regret leaving Pandro?"

"It is not that, Captain. Naturally I had no desire to remain and rule the planet. But there was something else the Tam Paupa offered which I cannot get out of my mind." He looked speculatively across at Kirk.

"It insisted in its own way of communicating that it could instruct me how to fully disassociate in the fashion of the Pandronians. The possibility of being able to separate my body into several independent sections was so intriguing that I confess for a brief moment I was sorely tempted."

"I'm glad you didn't accept, Spock," Kirk told him honestly, appalled at the picture his mind conjured up of three Spock sections running haphazardly about the ship. "I like you the way you are. In one piece."

"That was my eventual feeling also, Captain. Besides, while the Tam Paupa was positive it could teach me to disassociate, it was not quite so certain it could show me the way to reintegrate again. The only thing I want following me through the universe is my shadow. Not," he added strongly, "my arms or legs. I'd rather be a whole Vulcan than a parade."

"Amen to that," Kirk concurred. Then his mood turned somber as the viewscreen replaced the receding planet Pandro with a spacious view of stars and nebulae.

"You know, the Klingons with their experimental creatures weren't behaving much differently than children do with building blocks. Their toy just got out of hand at the end." He stared at the vast panorama on the screen, which formed a very tiny portion indeed of one infinitesimally small corner of the universe.

"In a way we're all like Captain Kor and his people—children playing with building blocks that we don't always understand. We have to be careful and keep the castles we build out of them down to sizes we can manage, or one day they're all liable to come tumbling down on us. . . ."